LINDA KLEINDIENST

Books by André Schwarz-Bart

A WOMAN NAMED SOLITUDE

André Schwarz-Bart

A WOMAN
NAMED
SOLITUDE

TRANSLATED FROM THE FRENCH
BY RALPH MANHEIM

Atheneum   *New York*
1973

For you, without whom this book would not be—nor my life

The mulatto woman Solitude was with child at the time of her arrest; she was executed on November 29, 1802, immediately after the delivery of her child.

Oruno Lara,
Histoire de la Guadeloupe,
Paris, 1921

PART ONE

BAYANGUMAY

1

Once upon a time, on a strange planet, there was a little black girl by the name of Bayangumay. She had made her appearance on earth about 1755 in a calm and intricate estuary landscape, where the clear water of a river, the green water of an ocean, and the black water of a delta channel mingled—and where, so it is said, the soul was still immortal.

But the inhabitants of this region had no Olympus, no Valhalla or heavenly Jerusalem. They were not inclined to lose themselves in the clouds, for they were too much attached to their cows, their salt meadows, and most of all to their rice paddies, which were known and prized throughout West Africa. Three days after their funerals they simply went down to the Kingdom of the

Ancestors, which was under the village, three feet
below the surface, and they all knew where to
find it. The living brought them offerings, fed
them with sacrifices, poured palm wine for them
into the holes in the ground that served as altars.
In exchange for which the departed helped them
with their farming, blew into the roots of plants
as though playing flutes, to give the rice its secret
music and make it prosper. They dwelt underground for one or two generations, according to
the degree of their weariness with life, their lone-
liness or boredom; then, rising through the roots
of a tree, they would lurk in wait for a passing
woman and gently slip into her. Thereupon they
became *lizard babies*, and a few months later, if
nothing went wrong, they resumed their place in
above-ground society. Thus their death was a kind
of life, their life a rebirth, and they regarded
themselves as the owners in perpetuity of their
cows, their lovely salt meadows, and their marvelous rice paddies.

At birth Bayangumay bore a strawberry, or
rather blackberry, mark on the still-milky skin
of her belly. When they saw it, the Elder Women
wagged their heads and smiled knowingly. And
while the men put the placenta in the ground and

beside it planted a tree to which the child's destiny would be attached, the old women decreed that the child would bear the name of Pongwé, her late maternal grandmother, since she was manifestly her reincarnation. But since the child had long eyelashes, so fine that they lay flat on her eyelids, she was also given the made-up name of Bayangumay, which in the Diola language means: she whose eyelashes are transparent.

From earliest childhood the little girl dreamed of her grandmother Pongwé, who had been the reflection of an earlier grandmother, who in turn had been the reflection of a still earlier grandmother, and so on, and so on, like the successive images that appear on the surface of a river and are carried away by the current only to be reborn. Bayangumay herself was one of these images carried away by the current, and one day no doubt she would make way for a little girl who would be just as interesting as today's little girl, with the same nose, the same eyes, the same shoulders shivering in the wind, the same bluish-black strawberry, or rather blackberry, mark on her belly; who would bend over in the same way to caress all sorts of thoughts in the mysterious, forever changing waters of the river. At this point in her daydreams she was always filled with a delicious dizzy exaltation. But on some days there was a distant pain at the bottom of her joy, and she wondered why her grandmother's voice never spoke to her, why in her heart she heard only the frail voice of Bayangumay. Her mother comforted her, reminding her of the mark that was still visible next to her belly button, and assuring her that all her gestures, all her facial expressions and modulations of speech were definitely those of her grandmother. And besides, she concluded with a smile, even this obstinate profusion of silly questions undoubtedly had its source in the poor heart of the woman Pongwé—peace to the whiteness of her bones.

Then, somewhat bewildered, her forehead creased with doubt, the little girl went off in silence and wandered about on the fringes of the village, asking herself how it came about that she felt so strongly, so ardently, so exclusively Bayangumay. How was it possible that she should look upon the land of men as though she had never seen it? That at every moment it seemed so prodigiously new to her? That she recognized nothing in the world where she had lived long ago, in her previous existences?

* * *

On the day of her birth she had been promised
to Dyadyu, an old friend of her father's, in memory of a hunting expedition they had gone on together in the mountains of Mahor in the lamented
days of their youth, before the trails were set
with man traps. Dyadyu lived in Énampore,
where the rain kings are chosen, and he swore by
the waters that he could not accept this favor,
for he would be too old, if not dead, before the
girl's loins had ripened. But he had to give in,
for fear of offending his old companion of the
hunt. He set his hope in death; he hoped to die
before the girl's hips were rounded, for he was
not one of those who eat valikalam root to uphold
the glory of their member. But the evening wind
carried away his words, and he was still firm on
his legs when Bayangumay was given her second
surname, Utili bän ulin, which in the Diola language of the riverbanks means: You are fat but
your weight does not impede your movements.

When Dyadyu went to visit his young betrothed
in her family enclosure, he pinched the child's
arms, her plump thighs, and the ever so delicate
fluting of her ribs. Dyadyu was able to make
presents and had the art of choosing them: clay
dolls, yo-yos made from mangoes, little bells, tops
carved from tiny lemons, bead bracelets, and gir-

dles for her future nights as a woman. Then Bayangumay would curtsy, raise an indecipherable
face half hidden by her parted fingers, and with
secret pleasure accept the gifts of this man who
would soon be her husband and whom she had always addressed as Betrothed, just as she said
Uncle to all those who called her Niece. All in all,
she was rather pleased with her position in life.
Betrothed as she was to a notable, the grown-ups
looked upon her as one of their own, though her
limbs had not yet attained the requisite length.
That gave her a slightly dizzy feeling, as when,
her body bristling with feathers, she hopped about
on dancing stilts on the night of the King of
Énampore's birthday. But some of the things she
heard brought her down from the heights. The
little boys said that through her Dyadyu only
wanted to marry her late grandmother Pongwé.
It seemed there had been a romance between them
—a sad story. But he would surely be dead before
she saw her menstrual blood, and they would have
to wait underground for another reincarnation.
. . . Oh, how many moons would pass before
Dyadyu could at last be wedded to the beautiful
Pongwé! . . . Malicious tongues said this and
more. But strange to say, such words flattered the

soul of Bayangumay, and although she pretended
to take offense, this too made her feel pleased with
her rather acrobatic position on the mysterious
and unstable ladder of incarnations. The only
one who really troubled her was Komobo, a little
boy of commonplace appearance, with pointed
ears and eyes that feigned innocence. Komobo
never said belly words like most little boys whose
stem is rising, but on his lips even the most innocent expressions became obscure, insidious, and
most unpleasant. Of all the nicknames in the
world he had no doubt found the only one capable
of wounding the heart of Bayangumay. He had
used it since their earliest childhood. At every
opportunity he would sidle up to her with an air
of detachment and whisper one word in her ear,
always the same: crayfish. He also had a way of
approaching in little jumps, with an occasional
lurch sideways, in imitation of the crayfish's gait.
And when such cavorting was forbidden because
of some ceremony or solemn rite, he would quietly
raise his arms over his head in such a way as to
suggest the feelers of the little blue crayfish that
abound in the Balanta country. Once during a
funeral when the grown-ups showed their dis-
pleasure at this performance, Komobo had a new

idea: Assuming an attitude of perfect immobility,
he would make his eyeballs pop out until they
were as round and protuberant as the little globes
on a crayfish's head. Then he would speak of some
fish he had eaten the day before at his family
board and the little girl would be overcome with
shame. One day when she could bear it no longer,
she suddenly retorted with the epithet of the pig:
"You whose flesh is made to be pickled." But far
from taking offense, Komobo put on the sweetest
of smiles, gazed at her with eyes of innocence, and
unleashed one of those surprise arrows of which
he possessed the secret: "Kawalong Kadyack,"
he replied with a smile. This was the most common epithet of the Wali Wali, or water hen, so
winsome to the eye and so tender to the mouth—
"Kawalong Kadyack," which in the language of
the riverbanks signifies: "How delicious are your
hind parts cooked with almonds."

This incident occurred beside one of the channels at the time of the morning chores. Kneeling
on the long flat stones, some ten children of the
same age group would plunge leaf baskets into
the green, night-cool water and then, deftly
swinging the baskets over their shoulders, empty
them into earthenware jars. Komobo's words rose

laughingly to the sky, there were giggles and pointed smiles. Bayangumay lifted her jar to her head and gravely made her way to the family enclosure. For several days she remained within it, silently dreaming of all the things that could happen in the land of men: lots of little boys fell from the crowns of palm trees, stung by a palm wine snake; some dried and shriveled up, some swelled like water skins; others got lost in the woods and disappeared no one knew where, sold perhaps to the white djinns of Sigi-Thyor—why couldn't such a thing happen to Komobo? Why? . . .

One day Komobo's belly swelled up and the little girl knew how gravely she had sinned. Informed without delay, her first mother summoned all the women to meet the following day at a hut some distance from the village, which was the confessional of the clan. As custom prescribed, she told no one of the reason for the meeting. In order to preserve the mysteries of their sex, a number of novices kept a strict guard around the hut Some were even posted in the leaves of the trees nearby. When all the women had seated themselves inside, each in the place befitting her age, charisma, or ties with the spirit of the place, Bayangumay's first mother pushed her into the center of the circle and said: "Say what you have to say, and remember that the word holds up the building."

Bayangumay's head was bound with the white band of the penitent; her hands lay flat on her shoulders, her eyes were cast down and her face ravaged with fear. Erect in the center of the circle, she confessed that an evil spirit had taken possession of her heart. And when she was asked why she wished for Komobo's death, her poor little mouth opened in anguish but she did not speak. She trembled and moved her tongue like a fish gasping for air. Having asked leave to speak, Komobo's first mother tearfully put the questions that all the women were asking in their hearts. Still the child stood voiceless in the center of the circle. Her eyes, filled with a dreamlike desperate expectation, rolled slowly in their sockets. Two priestesses approached her and, having decided that she was searching sincerely, intoned the traditional song of the boekin of woman's confession. Their voices were discordant, each apparently trying to show its special virtue by rising higher than the other. Their owl's eyes glittered and at

length they cried out in tones of command:
"Elana, Elana, you, the first man, you who rent
your limbs and shed your blood to give us a land
and waters, light up this child's heart, light up
this heart, Elana. . . ."

Suddenly touched by the spirit of the boekin,
Bayangumay, trembling from head to toe, entered
into the motions of the slow, revolving dance of
those who have seen their sin. A fine foam oozed
from her lips and unaware of what she was saying
she murmured in a shrill nasal voice that was the
voice of the boekin: "Because he holds me far
from his joy, oh, how far . . ."

No sooner had these words been heard than a
sigh went up from the assembly; several of the
old women exchanged smiles and their oiled eyelashes fluttered with astonishment. . . .

2

THE SWELLING in Komobo's belly went down, but a sort of interdict was imposed on the two children: They were obliged to disregard each other, for that was the Diola rule. But they belonged to the same age group, and the children's work, play, and ceremonies still brought them together. A subtle dialogue, spoken and unspoken, was woven between them over the crinkled heads of their comrades. Words were tossed negligently into the air and fell with the imponderable precision of a dream, like those long flat stones that skip so well, rising and falling on still water. The word crayfish had fallen into disuse, for crayfish had become a rarity now that the fishermen had stopped going to the Balanta country for fear that they themselves would be caught in the nets of the fishers of men. But there was no lack of words alluding to the ponds, rivers, and channels, and to the innumerable beasts of the sea, and in those days woven of innocence poor Komobo became so enthusiastic about fishing that he was nicknamed An Asulène, which signifies: hungry for fish.

One evening under a little green moon as taut as a bow the whole age group was gathered under their usual mandarin tree, exhausted after a day spent transplanting rice. Not far off a few grown-ups were singing the vigor of their blood, the beauty of the rice to come, and the kindness of the moon that favored their song. A tom-tom breathed lightly under the fingers of a man who was wandering about mumbling no one knew what, drunk with sleep. From time to time a little girl arose with an absent look, threw back her head, and, her face filled with a sacred fury, kneaded the ground with her little pink heels. She waved her arms wildly, seeming to struggle against an immense wave, and then passively let herself be led to a boy who had entered the circle with the same absent eyes. Bayangumay emerged from the shadow; her shoulders flapped like wings, but her torso, glistening with palm oil, was straight and still. As she floated over the ground, one with the beating of the drum, everything she loved and everything she feared dissolved in the ocean of the world. Suddenly, without a thought, she stopped still in front of Komobo and, shivering like a blade of grass, sang in the mocking manner of the old women:

Handsome boy, lead me.
Dance; shine under the moon like a silver fish.

The little girl had danced the dance of the trembling shoulders for Komobo, and everyone knew it. After that they were watched and Dyadyu was notified. He smiled and brought presents, as though nothing had happened. Soon Bayangu-may's belly burst and the blood rained down her thighs. She was a woman, it was time to think of marrying her. When pressed, Dyadyu turned a deaf ear: The fruit was still a bit green for his teeth. The rumor went around that the children were seeing each other in secret and that the betrothed had lost her ring. Dyadyu's reluctance was interpreted as disapproval of the silent friendship between Bayangumay and Komobo. Called upon to carry out his promise, Dyadyu replied with a smile that there would be no virtue in it.

16

Taking a little water in the hollow of his hand, he said to Bayangumay's father: "Which is pure, old friend . . . this water that has just come out of the ground, or this hand that has lived for fifty years? . . . Ever since she was born I have known all Bayangumay's thoughts, for she is as clear as this water in the horny hollow of my hand."

"Today," said a member of the Council of Elders, "I heard an intelligent word." And he clicked the flat of his lips with satisfaction.

Bayangumay's first mother was a secretive woman, rough-mannered and cool-headed, well known for never following her own pathways. "At the beginning of time," she liked to say, "no paths had been laid out in the land of men, you couldn't go anywhere; but little by little, where the Ancestors passed, paths were opened. And on those paths," she concluded with a menacing air, "we set our feet in gratitude." Some days before the date for her marriage was fixed, Bayangumay heaved a long sigh, and complained in these terms: "You threaten me, you examine the ring of my virginity; but for the last three years I haven't said a word to Komobo. And I've danced with him only once." Her first mother rubbed her

teeth with a stick of lemon wood and replied drily:
"Exactly. That was one dance too many; the first
time the she-ape climbed a tree, everyone saw
that her behind was bare."

"Ever since I was a little girl," said the child,
"I have been preparing myself to become Dya-
dyu's wife. And everything I do is taken amiss.
Shame on your thoughts, I say."

Her mother studied her with a cold eye and
said:

"Do you mean to argue with the Ancestors?"

"No," said Bayangumay.

"Then remember that all we who live draw our
life from those below. And so do you, for you are
the reincarnation of my mother, who was as crazy
as you are—I say this to both of you, because
I've had plenty of trouble with you both. When
anyone rebels against the living, it's as if he were
trying to defeat the dead and the spirit of Elana
himself, who feeds the living and the dead and the
boekin. I tell you both, you and my mother's
spirit that is in you, as plain to see as the shape
of your ears: No one can rebel against the law,
because the law itself obeys the law."

Bayangumay was sitting on a stone. She
watched the sun shining in the sky, then paling

and going down at the offense that had been done
him.

At nightfall she went secretly to the woods, hid
a blanket, some toilet articles, and a basket containing rice, pepper, salt, and dried fish. Then
she slipped into Komobo's hut and told him to
meet her late that night in the first forest clearing. "That's not possible," he said. "You've been
drinking from the madwoman's gourd." "It may
not be possible for you," she said coldly. "I shall
wait for you until morning, then I shall know
whether you've thought it possible or not." For a
long time she waited patiently. At last she saw
Komobo coming. He was wearing his feast-day
attire and had his hunting and fishing equipment.
On his neck, arms, wrists, waist, and thighs he
wore copper rings and war rattles filled with seeds
muffled by wads of grass. From his belt hung bells,
a sheathed knife, a small wooden club, and an
ornate flute. On his head he wore a cap made of
cowrie shells, surmounted by a woolen pompon
and a red feather that glittered in the moonlight.
He was going to his death, to his own funeral.
Tears came to Bayangumay's eyes and, quickly
picking up her basket of rice, she said tenderly:
"Komobo, Komobo, if you take all the colors, what

19

will be left for the birds?" The boy hesitated for
a few minutes. "Maybe," he said. "Maybe we
ought to go back and say goodbye to our village?"
And when the little girl did not seem to agree, he
protested half-heartedly:

"Your thoughts are a fog to me. . . ."

Gliding quickly into the shadow, they went to
the river where Bayangumay caught sight of a
splendid child-size canoe. According to the itinerary she had planned, they would have to cross
the delta, the watery tresses of the Casamance, ex-
tending from the sea to the hills where the Balanta
country begins. A good many of its channels were
forbidden them—some because they passed
through Manjak territory, others because sacred
fish, manatees, crocodiles, and hippopotami lived
in them, and still others, narrow and bordered by
mangrove swamps, because the sellers of men
infested them by night. In the deforming moonlight, it seemed to the two children that they
were paddling through the land of the dead. The
night passed in silence, the boy paddling and
the little girl standing in the stern, guiding the
canoe with a pole. Komobo's back glistened with
fright.

Bayangumay said:

"Komobo, Komobo, why did you call me cray-fish?"

And he answered without turning around:

"Have you ever seen a living crayfish?"

"No," she said.

The last channel ended in a mangrove swamp. The leg-shaped roots of the trees grew high above the ground. The two children set foot in the mud and Bayangumay was amazed at this forest of legs. Bent by the wind, they all leaned in the same direction like groups of dancing girls frozen in mid-flight, and some resembled certain of the village girls with their smooth melodious lines and a grace that seemed to be of another world. But at the base of all this magical beauty the eye discovers the black mud swollen with bubbles; and suddenly Bayangumay, grown thoughtful, asked her companion:

"Komobo, Komobo, are you sure of being your paternal great-uncle?"

Dreamily and very gently he murmured:

"What would you expect me to be, my great-aunt?"

"I don't know, I don't know. . . ."

Guiding their canoe across the mangrove swamp, they came to the tall grass. There they left it and climbed a hill fissured by a deep stream of fresh water. When the dawn came, they were halfway. Komobo unrolled the blanket on the sand and laid his dashiki over it to soften their bed. "But where will you lie?" Bayangumay asked. Then Komobo picked up his dashiki with resignation and laid it down in the tall grass not far away. Arrows of fire shot from the line where heaven and earth met. Sitting on his holiday dashiki, Komobo baited a trap, then he went down to the brook. In a little while he came back and lay down shivering.

When Bayangumay awoke a few hours later, the sun had risen from the realm of the dead to warm the living. She saw Komobo sitting not far off, as solemn as a madman and as calm as a man about to die. "Come," he said to her. She followed him to the brook, where he picked up the trap, uncovering a small crayfish, which he tossed into the grass. The Balanta crayfish was indeed blue, a shiny opalescent night-blue. And the rings of its body resembled the folds on the neck of a girl who is rather fat, but whose weight does not impede her movements. "Utili bän ulin," said Komobo. The girl smiled, picked up the crayfish and tossed it back into the water. They both burst out laughing.

And so they passed three days on a hill in the Balanta country, talking little and about many things.

On the morning of the third day she said: "Komobo, I must go to my wedding." And vainly trying to read her thoughts, the boy replied: "I am afraid Dyadyu will kill me." At length he heaved a sigh and they went down the hill to the canoe they had hidden in the tall grass.

When they reached Énampore, Dyadyu was waiting in the open square, surrounded by the men of his clan. He had put on his great indigo dashiki—the warrior's ceremonial dress and winding sheet. He had rubbed his teeth with lemon wood, so setting off his incisors, which had been filed to points. He bore no weapon except for his short battle sword and no ornament except for his cap of cowrie shells, which had been sewn to his gray hair and looked like tiny sun-bleached jawbones. The arrival of the runaways unleashed a tempest of cries, shouts, and strident squeals, most of which emanated from the women of Énampore. One of the men of Dyadyu's clan hurled his spear at Bayangumay's father, who was waiting, erect and as stiff as a corpse among his kinsmen. Directed with precision, the point only pricked the skin of his ankle. All stood motionless. Those who were near the wounded man bent down to gauge the gravity of his hurt. Then one of them raised his weapon, took careful aim, and hurled it in such a way as to make an identical wound in Dyadyu's ankle. When one of his party lifted his spear, Dyadyu said without raising his voice: "Whosoever throws a dart will die by my hand."

At this moment the anger of the crowd, which had been diverted for a moment, turned back to Bayangumay. Fists were raised, insults rained from all sides, the little girl was seized with the same feeling as three days before; standing before the people, raising herself to her full frail height, she sang the song she had composed during her absence:

> We have passed three days on the hill
> A little canary in its box
> No more than I thought of it
> Did Komobo think of it
> Komobo is not a tainted boy
> Nor is he a young man of our times
> Kilili, Komobo. Kilili
> Let the tom-tom of Weili sing Komobo

Then she went to Dyadyu and knelt before him with hands joined and elbows far apart, in token of perfect submission; but she held her head high and her eyes were turned toward the glittering sky.

The old man laid his left hand on Bayangumay's round little head to show that he had heard her words and her song. Then he touched her shoulder, signifying that she should rise from her fault. And while the circle narrowed around them, he asked in a courteous tone: "How did you eat?" She replied. Then: "How did you sleep?" She replied. Then: "I see that your hair is still damp; how did you bathe?" She replied. And at length: "Did one of you touch the other?" She answered: "We did not even touch each other's hands."

Dyadyu spoke in a grave, penetrating voice, and his face seemed perfectly calm amid the angry faces of his clan. Still, there were clouds in the sky of his gaze. Suddenly Bayangumay was afraid. Unwittingly she began to make little whimpering sounds, though her head remained erect and her eyes fixed on Dyadyu, who seemed to drift away into a dream in the midst of the crowd that was waiting for his verdict. Everyone knew that this man's words were acts, that they could take the form of a spear, an arrow, or a hurled knife. Bayangumay's first mother slumped to the ground, poured a handful of sand on her disheveled hair, and, hiding her face between her knees, let out a piercing scream. Her kinsfolk surrounded her and tried to quiet her. Then Dyadyu seemed to return to himself, to the present moment, to his people, and with a strange, appeasing smile he looked into the pink whites of Bayangumay's eyes and uttered the old proverb: "The heart of man is an inconsolable child." Then he fell silent.

The meaning of this proverb, reserved by custom to the Elders, was obscure. Yet, though she did not understand them, the ancient words pierced Bayangumay's heart, and stricken with grief she threw herself at Dyadyu's feet. Dyadyu asked for some branches. When they were brought to him, he struck Bayangumay's shoulders three times, as a father strikes a child who has committed some slight offense, vigorously but with tenderness. Then he made her get up, laid his hand on her shoulder in token of protection, and said: "To me it is all clear, but we must still question the Spirits." And he pushed her ahead of him through the crowd. When a young man smiled as they passed, Dyadyu gave him a punch that laid him out on the ground. The witch doctor led them to his hut. Bayangumay went down on her knees and the witch doctor placed a white hen on her head to determine the state of her virginity. The hen's claws scratched her scalp a little but soon came to rest. The witch doctor said: "All is well, she is straight. She has only made a little noise. You will have a noisy wife."

Old Dyadyu smiled: "Even as a child she was a flute which her ancestors played all day long."

Then he added:

"For the sound of her body is clear."

Bayangumay was lying in the half-light. She felt that she was floating on palm wine, on the many dances she had danced, on the drowsy note of the tom-tom that came to her from far off, from the middle of the village. A cotton wick was smoldering in the doorway, where Dyadyu would soon appear. She knew they were making him ready as they had made her ready; the older wives had washed the sweat of the dance from her body; they had rubbed her with fresh tulucuna oil, which gave her skin the strong smell of her first mother. Then they laid her down on a mat, put a white loin cloth on her, placed her legs in the right position, and folded back a corner of

the loin cloth to disclose her nakedness, in order
that everything might be exactly right to receive
the man. Against her loins she felt the girdle that
children never see. They only hear its tinkling,
and shake pebbles between their hands in fun.
Freshly oiled, Dyadyu appeared in the doorway.
"Is my wife ready?" he asked in a tone of deference. It occurred to Bayangumay that the old
warrior would never again call her "my child,"
and at the thought she was suddenly filled with
shame and sadness and regret. Dyadyu made a
slight movement and said:

"I could come back in a little while if you are
not yet ready to receive me; for I am no longer
a young man who flings himself at the first doe.
All my impatience is behind me. . . ."

Bayangumay smiled in the half-light:

"But all mine is before me," she said.

"All?" said Dyadyu with a soft laugh, and
snuffed out the wick between his fingers, abandon-
ing the hut to the impalpable glow of the night.

She had thought she detected a dark note in
his laugh and her heart swelled with a strange
feeling as she tensed her arms and thighs so as
to withstand the test with all the strength of her
body. A light sigh, still charged with the same
sadness, escaped her, and seeing that the man

was bending over her she compliantly raised her
loins, lifting the sacred corner of her body as
high as she could, just as Dyadyu's three old
wives had taught her. She was the victim and the
altar; it was her duty to stretch like a bow, to
offer the middle of her body like a sacrificial
animal freely offering its neck to the knife.
Dyadyu uttered the ritual words: "May the rice
we planted this year grow in abundance and
vigor." And softly Bayangumay said the prayers
of the receiver, which the three old women had
just taught her, in order that the seed which gives
life to all things from the depths of the earth to
the stars might sprout within her. And when
everything was done that had to be done, when,
resting from his travail, Dyadyu lay upon her—
not with all his weight but only with the part of
it that he could not support on his elbows—she
said to him from deep down in her stifled throat:
"Dyadyu, Dyadyu, I thank you for making me
your wife." Dyadyu made no answer. The young
wife cast about for another formula and finally
let her own mouth speak: "Dyadyu, Dyadyu,"
she said. "My womb is honored to bear the seed
of such a tree as you." Still Dyadyu did not answer, and not with her ears but with her breasts,
which were pressed to the old man's chest, she

heard deep within him a sigh that stirred with his breath. At this she felt crushed by his weight, as though the whole incomprehensible weight of the world rested upon her. And not knowing how to speak of so many things at once, the child wondered if it might not be possible to express her tenderness for the world in a gesture; but there was no part of Dyadyu's body on which she could set her hand without disrespect, neither his shoulders nor his head nor his neck with its throbbing vein. And suddenly, from deep down in her throat, she sang:

Dyadyu, Dyadyu
If I cry from afar he comes to my help
If I cry out with my tongue, he comes to my help
Beside my cheek
Dyadyu

And when her song had ended, she saw that Dyadyu had cast off his restraint and was lying on her with all his weight, his chest rising and falling slowly, calm and appeased, like the chest of a man asleep, though she knew that his eyes were open in the night: with what feelings, what thoughts as vast and mysterious as the world?

3

WHEN BAYANGUMAY WAS BORN, the big city on
the river, a place of shade and quiet luxury, still
bore the name of Sigi, which means: Sit down.
But then it became a slave port and was given the
name of Sigi-Thyor: Sit down and weep. And little
by little, from the known regions to the most distant, to the lands beyond the Balanta country, the
peoples who feared to be hunted became hunters,
forgetting that the wound in the flanks of hunters
and hunted alike was one and the same. The land
of real men writhed under the evil that had been
instilled in its blood. And the Elders likened the
new body of Africa to an impaled octopus losing
its substance drop by drop while its tentacles
squeeze and rend each other without mercy, as
though to punish each other for the stake that

traverses them all. Fleeing from the banks of the Casamance, the traditional path of the sellers of men, the Diolas gradually retreated to marshes that could be reached only with difficulty; certain groups had gone to the inhospitable Cajinoles, where in the dry season they fed on mangrove oysters roasted over the coals. Palisades of pointed tree trunks were built around the villages and even around the huts within the enclosures, for everyone distrusted everyone else. A new saying was heard throughout the region: "In the past we feared only our enemies; today we fear our friends, and tomorrow we shall fling our spears at our mothers."

The ultimate destination of the captives was unknown: The common people said the whites fed on human flesh; the sages believed they offered it up to their gods; those who felt their minds were cracking contemplated the immensity of the sky and said nothing.

One night Bayangumay woke with a start. Raising her eyelids, she knew she was still asleep, and at the same moment she knew that she was living a dream within her dream. The village was one outcry, one flame, which lit up the hut as in

broad daylight. In this nightmare that knew itself for a nightmare, she saw her aged husband
standing naked in the middle of the hut, his spear
upraised and his mouth open in a cry of horror,
while with his free hand he hid the shame of his
sexual parts. Then came a shattering sound like
the sound of thunder in the dry season, when the
sky cracks like a kernel of maize in the coals. Falling down on his knees, old Dyadyu thrust his
spear forward and lay down on the ground to
sleep, resting his head on the crook of his elbow
as men do by the fireside after days of plowing,
sowing, circumcision, marriage or funeral, when
everything that was to be done has been done. She
decided to say nothing, to tell no one of this dream,
for she knew she did not really desire her husband's death: The plowing would soon be over, and
she would be able to see Komobo; so why such a
dream at such a time?

She thought she had better sacrifice a white
rooster to the boekin to dispel the sin of her dream,
her offense against old Dyadyu, who now lay
asleep beside her on their marriage mat. A prayer
came to her lips: "O gods of my blood, remove
this dream from me." At that moment two spirits
of the night rushed into the hut howling and drove

Bayangumay out of it with their long metal sticks. They had beaks, clothes like plumage, and on their foreheads stars within silver crescent moons. In her haste, Bayangumay bumped into her husband's body. In the middle of his chest there was a hole very much like the mark of a rhinoceros horn. She let out a feeble howl and still howling ran to the crowd gathered under the conference baobab. She pushed through the crowd as through a living wall of mud, while somehow the spirits of the night unleashed abrupt storms traversed by lightning. The huts roundabout were flaming like torches, raining coals on the brusquely awakened and for the most part naked bodies: men, women, and children, grandfathers and gnarled old crones with pink scalps and sagging jaws. The spirits of the night goaded the crowd with their long curved knives; some of the children tried to run away, but if one of them left the circle a stick struck him down with thunder and lightning. Sounds were coming out of Bayangumay's mouth; listening, she discovered that she was muttering: "What is it? . . . what is it . . . what is? . . ."

As she turned her eyes in all directions, trying to understand the agitation of the women, the hysterical screams of the children, and the silence of the men who seemed imprisoned by their own gaze, she saw, a few heads away from her own, old Kobidja, guardian of the rain fetish, raise his two fists as smooth as polished wood to the sky. Suddenly he cried out with a nasal, swollen, inhuman voice that seemed to issue from the snout of a wart hog rather than from the mouth of a man: "Diolas, the gods are dead!" So saying, he leapt at a metal stick. Its lightning dug a hole in his belly and diffused a smell of burned flesh. A few war cries still rang out from deep within the village; now and then a gust of wind, buffeting the flames over one of the huts, revealed the silhouettes of men fighting. Beside her, Bayangumay, to her consternation, recognized the twisted features of Binta, her husband's first wife; she was clutching two children to her knees and breathing incomprehensible words. Bayangumay felt that it was absolutely necessary to find out what this woman was saying, for her dream had become so serious that she would be obliged to describe it in every detail in the morning. Respectfully laying her hand on Binta's shoulder, she asked her calmly: "Mother, what are you saying?" Terrified, without recognition, the other plunged her white eyes into Bayangumay's eyes, and went on making the same sounds, which suddenly turned out to be words: "Elana, all-powerful Elana," the poor woman repeated. "Protect us from the sellers of men!"

At that exact moment, as her dream was growing confused and taking on an appearance of reality, Bayangumay discovered that a whole basketful of little fish darts was coming out of her mouth and her two ears. And each dart was her own cry, regular and unceasing, that would die only with herself.

Death mowed the village square. Then the spirits attached the survivors to a long knotted rope and, slowly walking their saddle horses, guided the human file over the paths of servitude, now and then negligently slicing a weary head just above its wooden collar. This was the lot of those who were not sick, who were neither too old nor too young, and who allowed themselves to be shackled and collared.

A third of the captives reached the slave pens of Gorée, a small island sixty days' march northward, facing the Lebu town of N'dakaru. The cells were hewn out of the rock, rectangular holes opening on the eternal darkness of the corridors.

Every morning the night's corpses were taken out and thrown from a door overhanging the sea. They were replaced by new arrivals speaking new languages. Sometimes a muffled hum of singing and laughter reached the captives from overhead, from the upper floor where the white masters lived, accompanied by the swift beat of dancing feet and a scraping sound similar to that of the Diola violin. Then the music stopped, the walls closed in again, bodies became walls for other bodies, and life lost its contours, merging into something that has no name in the language of men.

One day cries rang out, unaccustomed sounds were heard, and the doors opened on an uncertain light that came from no one knew where. Black men rushed into the cells, removed the chains from the captives' necks and hands, leaving only those on their ankles, and pushed them out into a yard, where they were made to wash in enormous iron-hooped tubs. The touch of water was even more unbearable than the daggers of light; the strongest men reeled, whimpering like children. Trembling, Bayangumay fell on her knees before the tub. A miraculous respite followed, during which quantities of manioc, boiled meat, eggs, and kola nuts were distributed. Once again the captives

knew a human feeling, which may have been
shame, and like the others Bayangumay covered
her intimate parts with the flat of her hand. Time
passed. The prisoners ate and drank in silence,
stood up and sat down with an air of wonderment,
took a few steps, looked at the sky, the trees, their
brothers and sisters so near, so far, then mechani-
cally replaced a hand over their returning shame.
On the upper floor three white men, leaning on a
low iron railing, smiled as they looked down on
the cattle in the yard. Beside each one stood a
little black woman waving a fan. The movements
of these godlike men were serenely self-assured;
their garments shone with the colors of flowers,
rare insects, and birds; long blond curls hung
down over their shoulders, their teeth sparkled
white between their red lips, and the whole appa-
rition breathed an air of lofty indulgence and
kindness. . . .

Then the brief respite ended. Guards descended
on the yard. They had the brand marks of slaves
on their shoulders, but they acted with the impersonal brutality of masters. The prisoners were
fitted out with new rings and chains and shoved
back into the stone house, but not to their cells.
Instead they were driven with whips, iron clubs,

and rifle butts into a corridor leading down to the
sea. A three-master was anchored off shore and
small boats manned by sailors were rolling in the
swell at the foot of the cliff. A few yards away,
not far from the place where the night's corpses
were thrown, the snouts of sharks, curved like
fingernails, cleft the surface of the water. In tears
Bayangumay descended the little stone steps.
Ahead of her a captive raised his arm to hoist himself into the boat, then hesitated and stopped still.
It was an enormous Bambara, his cheeks streaked
with ritual markings. He had managed by stealth
to keep a little three-stringed guitar shaped like
the calao bird. Two white sailors tugged at his
shoulders and a black guard whipped him furi-
ously. He didn't budge. His two feet clung to the
last step, and his head revolved slowly on his neck
like that of a man asleep. Suddenly he leapt, pulling one of the sailors with him into the sea, clutching the sailor's neck with one hand while with the
other he held the strange little calao guitar. Men
shouted, shots were fired, and then there was a
great whirlpool traversed by red ribbons, quivering fins, and snouts leaping out of the water as
though pulled by the force of innumerable teeth.
Bayangumay hesitated, her head swayed as

though in a dream. Then she stepped into the boat and obediently lay down in the bottom.

At first she felt an agony of fear, a terror drunk on itself, which seemed at every movement of the waves to rise into the hot air. But this gave way to the torpor of her belly filled with manioc, the soft feeling of her limbs, which seemed swollen with water, suddenly saturated like plants in the first rains of the year. The solemn majestic joy of breathing an air as pure as perfume filled her with a wave of gratitude toward the unknown bodies lying on top of her, toward the wood under her cheek, and the tremulous waters beneath the boat, those waters which cradled the remains of the Bambara, surrounded the island of Gorée, and bathed the shores of Africa, now vanished forever.

The file of captives climbed a rope ladder and Bayangumay entered the white men's floating house, which was slowly taking the human cargo into its curved flanks. The deck hands were shouting and gesticulating, brandishing knives and metal sticks as though stricken with panic. Silently dragging their chains, the captives were herded into a hole dug in the middle of the ship. Some of the women staggered, moved their arms about like feelers, and advanced with the blind awkwardness of ants. Struck violently in the back, Bayangumay started to run. But at the edge of the hole her ankle chains caught in a cable and held her back for an infinitely sweet moment, during which her eyes took in the sky for the last time. She saw the tender flight of a gull and the unfurling of the great sails, which, it seemed to her, made a harmonious sound, at once dry and wet.

Dim lamps hung from the beams. The captives scurried through narrow passageways, crawled to the space assigned them, and lay down as best they could in the darkness of the unknown. The inside of the ship was a mysterious extension of the outside world. Vague outlines were prolonged into night skies, hills, trees, and animals. Bayangumay heard the click of the lock as her ankle was attached to the long crossbar, and already a shadow pressed against her body, just as she had pressed against the shadow that had lain down before her. Her head was swimming, she saw thousands of little fish squeezed into a belly, into a big living thing containing a heaven and an earth and dark whirling waters and a multitude of waves and bitter salt droplets. Then her eyes returned to the present: The last white man was climbing the ladder; first his torso, then his leather-sheathed legs passed through a circle of light. Then the light itself disappeared and nothing remained but indistinct sounds, slow, painful breathing faintly punctuated by the rattling of chains. The foul air, the smell of death imposed a new rhythm, cautious and miserly, on the breathers. In a half-dream Bayangumay extended her arm and discovered that there was not room enough to sit up in. Suddenly the air was filled with cries. Kinsfolk and fellow tribesmen were looking for each other in the darkness. Propped up on her elbows, Bayangumay cried out: "Men of the village of Seleki, I am Bayangumay, daughter of Sifôk and Guloshô boh." She waited a long moment, eager for a word of her native language amid the welter of foreign moans and cries. Then in a calm, matter-of-fact voice, as though addressing a neighbor in her home enclosure, she said several times: "Men of Énampore, I was the third wife of Dyadyu." Then abruptly she straightened her arms, stretched out quietly on her back and said so faintly that she could not hear herself: "Diolas, Diolas, isn't there a single Diola in this fish?"

Behind her head a faint light fluttered between

two planks, and by this trembling thread one
could guess that there was still a sky, an earth,
and even air. When the light went out, Bayangumay understood that the world outside was also
enveloped in night, and she wondered if there
were many stars. She dreamed that she was living
under a dead baobab stump and that her body was
the size and shape of a finger. She was suffocating
under the weight of the stump and the pervasive
smell of rot; but every time she tried to stand
erect and reach into the fresh air, she remembered
she was a worm and told herself not to be foolish.
If she could only shed one little tear, maybe it
would convince her that this body wriggling in
the night, this skin, these fingers, these blind eyes
still belonged to a Diola. But there was nothing
left under her useless eyelids, and from this she
inferred that the white men had sucked out her in-
sides as sorcerers do and replaced them with something that could not weep. When she woke up, the
smell made her think she was still living under the
stump. But then she saw the thread of light between the two planks just above her head, and she
vaguely knew that a night had passed. Around
her she heard feeble moans, hesitant, groping,
turned inward, like a sick body that has nothing

more to hope for. Here and there a moan ended in a clear, pure sob, and Bayangumay thought of the children who had been crowded into a cage in the bow of the ship. The cries were less frequent than the day before. Since everyone wanted to make himself heard, a rudimentary order established itself. Now and then a luminous Diola consonance detached itself from the darkness and chaos roundabout. But since Bayangumay knew she was a worm, the meaning of the words escaped her; the sounds were confused with her heartbeats. Somewhere a group of men were singing in a strange language. It seemed to her that she heard the vibrant Diola voice of Komobo. She was rather puzzled, because it was Komobo's voice and at the same time another voice that had never sounded in her ears. Long long ago she had thought she heard Komobo's voice through the walls of her cell on Gorée. But there was nothing childlike in today's voice, its tone was deep, almost hoarse; it was as though Komobo were singing with his belly rather than his throat, singing words utterly unknown to Bayangumay, which mingled with the stirrings of her blood and the irregular beating of her heart. . . .

Komobo's song was followed by a brief approv-

ing silence; and then another voice began to sing,
descending the slopes of slavery and death, singing the fall of man to the solemn accompaniment
of jangling chains. Over Bayangumay's head, no
more than an arm's length distant, chains were
beating against the floor with the fury of thunder,
and she wondered if men or women were shaking
them. Trembling as though with fever, she awoke
to her miseries—hunger, thirst, vermin, the lack
of air, the smell of others, and the smell of her own
feces that had escaped her during the night. Yes,
she was wholly human and alive again. Inspired
by this marvelous thought, she tried to swallow
her tongue. Some of the prisoners on Gorée had
managed it, and the dawn had found them cold
and dead in their chains. All you had to do was
curl the tip of your tongue and suck it back with
your breath, slowly, patiently, carefully, until it
entered the throat and blocked it. But whatever
people may say, a woman's tongue does not lend
itself very well to this exercise, and few women
succeed. Bayangumay would do it some day, oh
yes, she would do it. Even now, after only three
months of practice, she could reach the back of
her palate, she was approaching the gateway to
her windpipe and victory was not far off. But she

ought to cry out a farewell to Komobo, a last word
that would help him too to return to the shores of
Africa, where one day, underneath the land of
men, they would talk about everything as they
had done long long ago on the surface, in the
green hills of the Balanta country. How, oh how
was she to cross the barrier of shame and tell
Komobo she was there, without his seeing her ab-
ject state through the night?

Finally she composed a poem in her head and
attuned it to the rhythm and melody of the dirge
for the absent, o aké ombo aldhyuât: *oh, there is
someone whose smile effaces the darkness;* and taking advantage of a moment of silence, she sang in
her purest, most melodious voice, her voice most
resembling that of a woman:

> Oh, give me a message to take to the ancestors
> For my name is Bayangumay
> And tomorrow I will go away
> Yes, tomorrow I will cease to be an animal.

PART TWO

SOLITUDE

1

THE MÉTISSE SOLITUDE was born in slavery about 1772 on the French island of Guadeloupe: du Parc plantation, commune of Carbet de Capes-terre. The du Parcs used the Permanent Register system, which presupposes a stable economy, whose needs in men and horses do not vary. The list of "hands" had been established once and for all, and the names of the dead were transferred to the living who, when the time came, yielded them up with their souls. When an aged Rosalie died, she was buried without ceremony in a fallow field, a temporary cemetery, where her remains would fertilize the sugar cane in the years to come. And with her first outcry a new Rosalie would take her place on the plantation register.

She was almost white at birth, and it took her

six weeks to darken. In the small of her back she
had the pear-shaped, coin-sized mark common to
all métis; its color was the flaming purple of the
heavy, dangling banana blossom. In the course of
time, her skin became an acceptable brown, a supple envelope gliding softly over her muscles and
distilling a sweat hardly less glistening than that
of her black mother. The slaves saw the bastard
seedling as a sapodilla, an indigenous fruit with a
reddish skin and ambiguous bittersweet flesh, and
the child, whose mother in her amazement of the
first few days kept sniffing at her as if to compare
her with the fruit, her living symbol, did indeed
have the same smell, vaguely suggesting incense.
Bayangumay followed the contours of the little
face and found it hard to get used to them. Only
the mouth reassured her, because of the fullness of
the lips, which reminded her of Africa. Their
edges were delicately hemmed with alternating
black and white, the still discernible mark of their
Creator. What troubled the young mother most
of all was the eyes, one dark and one light-green,
as though belonging to two different persons.

The old saltwater blacks, rich in experience,
told her that this was what happened when the
mixture of bloods takes place too quickly and

without pleasure: in ditches, by the roadside, and especially on slave ships. For on a specified day, a month before the ship was due to reach port, the black women were washed in sea water and the drunken sailors allowed to make free with them. The children of the *pariade*, as this strange custom was called, often had conflicting features, eyebrows that could not make up their minds and eyes divided between two worlds. And that was the case with this poor seedling, this charming sapodilla, conceived on shipboard in frenzy and confusion.

But, said the old people kindly, let black Bobette be of good cheer: Her daughter's two eyes were one soul, and some of the masters, who were given to black flesh, would find them very beautiful.

When an article of this kind, worthy to wait on the master's table, was born, she was taken away before she could catch any of the often fatal diseases, or acquire the scaly hands and the turns of mind and speech characteristic of the cattle who worked in the fields. One morning, on the overseer's advice, she was carried off to the Big House to be brought up among the mulattoes who served as intermediaries between the blacks and the whites.

The woman who had been Bayangumay looked on with a cold eye as her child was taken from her. But a few days later, on her return from the fields, she wailed for a few moments at the sight of her little girl, whom they had brought back when it became evident that she was languishing for her mother's breast. All further attempts ended in the same way: A livid, voiceless, feverish child rejecting any breast other than that of black Bobette, as though—and so it was whispered in the huts of the New Niggers—the umbilical cord had not really been cut. Bayangumay despaired as she had done during her pregnancy, when night after night in her dreams she had seen a little white man with a whip in his hand coming out of her womb. But harsh measures and subtle stratagems proved equally useless. Every night, when her mother thought she had fallen asleep, the little creature crawled to her in silence and delicately clasped one of her legs.

On toward the child's fourth year, however, Bayangumay noted a slight improvement; little by little the child was becoming weaned from her mother's body, for now it was only the tip of her toe that she hugged and kissed.

2

OF ALL THE THINGS that move about on the earth
and in the sky, the most mysterious and charged
with meaning to the little girl's mind, the only one
indeed that really moved her, was Man (Creole
for *maman*) Bobette. Every night before falling
asleep, she reviewed the most surprising enigmas
of the day. Staring into the darkness, she saw the
slightest movements of the fabulous being who was
her mother, recalled every contraction of her features, and heard the lightest inflection of her
voice. And then she would concentrate very hard
in the earnest hope of penetrating Man Bobette's
secrets. This required severe concentration, which
a mere nothing could dispel: a scurrying rat, a
cry from a neighboring hut, her mother sighing as
she turned over on her bed of dry cane leaves.
Little Rosalie had a cool head on her shoulders

and was not to be sidetracked so easily. Once the alarm had passed, she resumed her delicate, exacting task, winding and unwinding the thread of her reverie. Night fell on her heart, and she was still at work when dreams clustering with dreams grew her slowly downward. Sometimes she woke up in the middle of the night, and half-smiling, half-troubled, asked herself: "Jesus and Mother Mary, what can there be in black Bobette's living body? What can there be in that woman? Rhoye rhoye rhoye, what? . . ."

She knew that her mother came from beyond the ocean, that she was a wilding, as the white men said, an African she-devil as the blacks called those who had not been born on the island and who could be recognized by the incisions on their faces, their animal language, and their alarming salt-water ways. Yet, though she was not freshwater-born, Man Bobette was not really a saltwater black: Apart from the curious shape of her incisors, there was nothing repulsive about her. And though the little girl kept watching her on the sly, she saw nothing to justify the annoying nickname of Congo-Congo. Some also called her the Mongoose and others the queen with the long breasts, as in the proverb. Actually Man Bobette re-

sembled all the old women who worked on the plantation, despite certain indications that she was
not as old as some of the others. Why was it that
in the fields there were only old and young, while
among the black women and particularly the
métisses who worked in the mansion house there
was also an intermediate class who were no longer
exactly young but were not yet old? It's all very
strange, thought little Rosalie. For her mother
was undoubtedly old like a ramshackle old hut,
with her ravaged skin and those splotches of gray
mold on her face, and on her body those tufts of
pink grass where the whips had fallen. Besides,
one of her ears was missing, which made her talk
on a slant, cupping one hand into a trumpet, like
the oldest of the old women. And then there was
the slight limp caused by her broken shinbone,
which had set wrong and still protruded in one
place, so that she walked like a mutilated insect,
a fly with one wing plucked off. She was old, beyond a doubt she was old. And yet—was that her
secret?—if you looked at her from a certain angle,
when she was asleep, for instance, in the half-
darkness of the hut, with her head resting on her
bad ear, she looked so young, with her almost
virginal profile, her unseen eyes, her mouth well

closed over the stumps of her teeth, that you
might have counted her among the youngest of
the young mothers on the du Parc plantation.
And sometimes when she was sitting, holding her
head and neck in the manner of a white woman or
métisse, she seemed so graceful (especially if the
sun hit her at the right angle) that little Rosalie
thought she understood why they called her the
queen with the long breasts, though actually her
bosom was as flat and furrowed as an old yam
field.

There was also a "secret" in her way of walking
some evenings as the hands were coming in from
the fields, with the overseer hurrying them along
and the dogs howling, they, too, impatient to get
back to their huts. Even on the saddest evenings,
when strong men, struck down by land and sky,
were carried back on stretchers, even then the old
black woman who was her mother could not help
pulling herself erect every three steps with a be-
wildering air of bravado and challenge that made
you forget her limp, her ravaged skin, her dry
eyes, and her almost hairless head . . . Yes,
whatever else she might be, the queen with the
long breasts she remained; a queen with secrets.
Perhaps . . .

* * *

Often in the midst of her reveries the child saw a man with Man Bobette—an old black with a wooden leg. Long ago, before the little girl was born, the dogs had caught him escaping up the mountain. Since he had the knack of sugar bleaching, the masters had only cut off his leg at the knee. The man came mainly on Sundays, at the hour when the field hands sat outside their huts between waking and sleeping, not knowing what to do with their idle limbs. Coming into the hut, he would put his hand on little Rosalie's head and pat her tenderly, just as if she had been a shining black child. But when he opened his mouth, it was always to talk about the little mulatto girls who start denying their mothers the moment their umbilical cord is cut. He muttered other words too, leaning close to Man Bobette, who seemed to tremble as she listened. But the child heard only what he had said about the mulatto girls. She went over to Man Bobette, knelt on one knee, and shook her head in protest. When she opened her mouth, only inarticulate sounds came out, and Man Bobette said to her with a smile: "Watch out. You're bleating again." And the child moved her tongue a second time, trying to pronounce the words that were stuck in her throat. Then she stood up in silence and solemnly went out to her usual place in the cane field. She plunged deep into the tall trembling stalks till she could no longer hear the sounds of the slaves' quarters. And there, bracing her feet firmly on the ground, tensing her naked body as though to dance, she screamed with all the strength of her arms and legs.

Yet in spite of his eccentricities and the pain they caused her, little Rosalie liked to think about the old black man with the wooden leg. He had about him a grave rigidity that moved her strangely. For instance, he took no interest in belly-wallowing, and no one had ever heard him say a word about what people do with their groins, mouths, and hindparts, as though they were pigs and couldn't tell them apart, not to mention the whites who were busy day and night inventing new kinds of belly-wallowing. No more than Man Bobette did the old peg leg ever mention such things. Nor did he ever say a word about the du Parc mansion. His eyes never turned toward the big white house with its colonnades and statues, whose lights in the evening could be seen going on one by one from the huts, which the masters had placed at the western foot of the hill lest the prevailing winds carry the lower smells to the upper nostrils. But on certain occasions, he said words that were almost as piercing as Man Bobette's silences. One such occasion had been the public execution of the Bambara wild woman who had thrust a needle into the skull of her newborn baby. They had tied her to the doorpost of one of the huts and coated her naked body with molasses. It took the manioc ants several hours to finish her off, and all that time, her eyes blazing like torches, she had screamed insults at the masters. Instead of sighing or compressing his lips like Man Bobette, the old peg leg had only murmured in his usual voice, the voice of a docile animal: "The masters are good, the masters are just, the masters are good, the masters . . ." The child had looked in amazement from the old man's placid face to Man Bobette's tight, impassive features, and suddenly discovered that they were both observing the scene with the same eyes: two little land crabs darting this way and that, searching, biting the air roundabout.

It was very hard to look at the world with such eyes. When you examined it coldly in this way, the claws of your eyes turned back into your head and tore it to pieces. The little girl had tried it a few days after the execution. But Man Bobette and

the peg leg always had those eyes under their in-
flamed eyelids, and no one on earth suspected it.
Sometimes you could make out the tip of a claw
in Bobette's eyes. But those of the peg leg were so
well veiled, so perfectly smooth that he had not
been whipped since he could remember. He came
and went on the plantation, gently putting down
his wooden leg, gently bending his back, gently
smoking his pipe, as though begging the masters
and overseers, the mulattoes of the big house and
the blacks of the canefields, even helpless old
women and naked little children for a word, a caress, a bowed head, and a supple backbone like
his own. At such times the whole man seemed to be
fashioned in the image of his pecker, where the
dogs had grabbed him long long ago on that fa-
mous day when they had caught him in the woods.
And when he sat huddled against the mud wall on
his one heel, his old white head seemed as sleepy
and woebegone as his old white pecker, innocently
displaying itself to the eyes of all who passed.

But sometimes little Rosalie, awakened late at
night by some noise, discovered Man Bobette and
the peg leg whispering in the light of an oil lamp;
and then the peg leg had crab eyes like Man
Bobette's, or perhaps even the eyes of the Bam-

bara wild woman, those eyes of flame, sulphur, and ashes that had insulted the masters more fiercely than the words that came out of her bleeding mouth.

Such mysteries give you plenty to think about in a dark hut shivering in the wind, somewhere on a little sugar island. . . .

One night distant voices traversed the darkness and little Rosalie pricked up her ears. But she lay still, not so much as a sigh escaped her, and she scarcely breathed, for fear of giving herself away. Her heart clanged like a bell, she was sure it could be heard far away in the night. How could Man Bobette and the peg leg fail to hear it? How could they be so deep in their secrets that such a din escaped them? "Strange," said little Rosalie to herself, as the pounding inside her changed to a delicate tinkling, to the anguished cry of a frog, to the peaceful lapping of a river bathing her limbs in its cold water.

Time passed. Now the child could hear the whispered words. The two friends had not lit the little oil lamp, and their voices and words seemed different. These were no longer the melancholy words that seep away into the night and lose themselves, as rain loses itself in the ground. These words were as hard and rough as stones, which the two huddled grown-ups seemed to be gathering into a pile. Soon the child heard the peg leg murmuring a slow, almost tuneless song, a song she had never heard before, the kind of song that could not be danced:

> We will walk in the night
> March in the darkness
> In pain and death

The song was so beautiful, there was so much gentleness in it, so much fear and quiet suffering that little Rosalie wondered if she were not dreaming it, if Man Bobette were not at that very moment asleep, lying on her bed of dry grass, while her little girl was wandering in a dream.

"Why march?" said the anxious voice of Man Bobette. "Why not lie down on the ground and end it once and for all? Why?"

The peg leg spoke with the same restraint, the same slow ceremony as he had put into his song:

"I've told you a hundred times, black woman; we're not here to be the white man's oxen. The Gods of Africa sent us to take possession of this country. All those who obey the voice of the Gods will take the boat back; and the oxen who lick the wood of their yokes will serve the masters in heaven as they have on earth."

"That's not what the freshwater niggers say," Bobette protested sorrowfully. "I know their language is putrid, but maybe they know these things better than we do. And they say the exact opposite. They say that bad niggers like us will be harnessed to plows and serve the masters for all eternity. . . .

"And anyway," she concluded in a voice so faint that the little girl had to repress a cry, "what is this boat?"

"The boat is death," said the old peg leg.

There was a long silence and then, as though by prearrangement, the voices of the old man and the old woman, a trickle of salt water and a trickle of fresh water, joined, almost inaudibly, in one of those songs that grown-ups never sing in public and that even children, in the vague fear of some great punishment, hum only in spite of themselves:

> Odidilo
> The boat is in the woods
> Let us get in
> Let us get in

Then there was another silence, still longer than the first, one of those dark silences in which secrets germinate, and then Man Bobette's voice spoke:

"Dear black man, your mouth breathes the truth, but some are warmed and some are burned by the same fire. Maybe those who still have a nation or a village will be able to take the boat back; but those whose nation no longer exists, whose village has been destroyed and whose ancestors are dead—where will they go, my good friend?"

"Peace," said the peg leg calmly. "Here we learn that our country is bigger than our village; here even those who have a village learn to forget it. Peace, I say, for my country is no longer in my village."

"Peace," Man Bobette sobbed. "But where then is your country?"

A flame flared in the darkness, lighting up the face of a young black girl with a long swaying neck and features like a doe. Glittering tears fell from her eyelashes like pearls from a broken necklace. Then the light moved and the child saw the old man put down his fingernail on the black skin of his forearm in a gesture that she had seen dozens of times in the course of her short life. It was the *color sign*, which for the whites, blacks, and mulattoes of the du Parc plantation summed up all things here below.

"This is my country," he said simply.

At that moment the child cried out with fright and the others turned around. Again the hut was engulfed in darkness. She heard the light step of Man Bobette, who knelt down and laid her hand by turns on the little girl's eyes, on her mouth, and on her pounding heart; and then without a word she began to strike her, aiming chiefly at the buttocks, back, and belly. Man Bobette struck with mechanical regularity, abruptly stopping from time to time to murmur in a sullen voice, heavy with homesickness, "*Aïe, this flesh thinks only of betraying. . . .*" This way of beating her was most unusual, and the little girl gave the matter serious thought. Ordinarily Man Bobette confined herself to the clothed parts of her body, for the masters didn't like the little mulatto girls to be damaged, especially their precious faces. When very little, Rosalie had taught herself to bear her mother's assaults in silence, in the hope, the vain hope, of sparing her a flogging. But today the bony fists struck new territory, the forbidden regions of the neck and cheeks, and Rosalie wondered why this sudden savagery, this lack of restraint. Maybe Man Bobette was trying to push her underground and despaired of succeeding. Maybe. An endless time passed, a timeless time that seemed composed of thirst, sun-baked stones, and a river flowing through the blue leaves of tall trees. Finally the old peg leg's voice was heard, the rain of blows ceased, and the world was like a smooth silent beach in the night. Half-smiling, half in anguish, the child asked herself: "What can be the matter with black Bobette today? Jesus and Mother Mary, what can there be in that woman's living body? Rhoye, rhoye, rhoye, what can . . ."

It was the same the next day and the day after and the days that followed. Man Bobette seemed to be seized with frenzy. She struck harder and harder, with that same stubborn, unfathomable look on her face. But one night when she awoke, little Rosalie felt that her mother was lying beside her, crying and stroking her hair. She would have liked to say something, to take her mother's hand, but she was too frightened. She knew she was falling asleep under her mother's caress. She tried hard to stay awake, but she couldn't.

When the child woke up, a few threads of light were interwoven with the roof thatch. The hut seemed very small. She sat up and looked at Man

Bobette's empty corner: a scattering of dry leaves, nothing more. By that time, no doubt, the two of them, Man Bobette and the old peg leg, were halfway up the mountain, climbing, slipping, falling, and picking themselves up again, clinging to everything there was to cling to, with only one thought; to get as far as possible before the dogs were unleashed. In the middle of her daydream the overseer burst into the hut. As he was expertly twisting her arm, she smiled inwardly, thinking: Dead flesh feels no iron. When he had gone, she shook her hair, shook the twigs from her smock, and rinsed her mouth with a little water. Looking around, she saw three little black heads in the doorway, watching her with interest. She followed them to the hillock at the edge of the cane field, the better to hear the dogs that were already bounding up the first slopes. On the opposite side the sun was emerging from its bath, shaking droplets into the sea. The three children started a game. Some black women, she thought, must take their children with them to the mountains, and then they take the little boat to Congo Island together. Grave and dry-eyed, she made the movements of a white man's dance, a little minuet step, saying softly to herself: "It's the same as if I cried out, the same as if I cried out."

67

3

THE CAREER of Louis Mortier had been marked
out by his father, a former *engagé* in the service
of the founders of the du Parc dynasty, who at the
end of the seventeenth century had not yet come
by their three roundels gules with an azure
label. Their herd consisted of some thirty Africans and a handful of European niggers, as the
white field hands were sometimes called. The du
Parc fortune had its origin in a contract signed
in 1700, whereby the Compagnie de Guinée under-
took to supply eleven thousand tons of black flesh.
At the time the du Parcs were small slave traders
at Basse Terre. Having got wind of the affair,
they invested and made a good thing of it; coat
of arms and title of nobility followed.

Mortier Père had been a poor peasant from the

Beauce region. Groaning under the weight of the corvée, he had not let himself be discouraged by the sinister reputation of contract labor in the colonies: eighteen months of slavery on the same footing as the Africans, in return for the ocean crossing and freedom at the expiration of the contract. The hitch was that no great effort was made to keep the *engagés* alive for more than eighteen months, whereas the African slaves, an inalienable capital often amortized in less than two years, had a good chance of lasting as much as six or seven. Mortier Père had horrendous tales to tell. True, he was speaking of a heroic, long past era, when niggers were rare and the Caribs were already beginning to die out. Nevertheless, his stories terrified the son, who swore to die in the skin of a landowner. As a very young man he tried his hand at coffee growing like everyone else, but one fine day the precious elixir became so abundant in Europe that the poor began to drink it for breakfast. The bottom fell out of the market, and Mortier was ruined. The three niggers who had cost him their weight in gold were virtually worthless. Then sugar came in. But it required large holdings and expensive equipment that only the big concessionaires could afford. The small

whites sold their parcels of land. As sugar pros-
pered, the price of niggers went up, but it was too
late. Louis Mortier was reduced to becoming the
du Parcs' agent and general manager.

A few years later the du Parcs removed to
Paris and carved out careers for themselves in
the magistracy and the army. Louis Mortier set
himself up at the "château" and informed them
of the state of their affairs in monthly reports
that crossed the seas irregularly, as the wind, the
waves, and the English, whose competition had
taken the drastic form of warfare, permitted. In
one of these reports, dated January 13, 1771, he
announced the acquisition of three males and two
females in replacement of some hands who had
passed on. He had his doubts about their value,
for the merchandise had been gravely impaired
by the crossing. For all his experience, he wrote,
he had been deceived in a nigger girl of sixteen,
who was probably epileptic. She had collapsed,
screaming and foaming at the mouth in the middle of the Basse-Terre market, just as he was in-
specting her openings for fear of the pox, the
green death, and other plagues she might easily
have acquired along with the bastard with which

she was definitely pregnant. M. Mortier expressed the hope that she would last until her
confinement, which would compensate for her
probable loss. A few weeks later he announced
that she was apparently not epileptic. But it had
been found necessary to keep her tethered and
above all isolated because of the bad example she
set by her unseemly behavior, swallowing her
tongue, eating pebbles, and even trying to stran-
gle herself by tugging at the iron bar that had
imprudently been affixed to her neck. For fear of
lockjaw, which was then raging on the plantations, M. Mortier supervised her confinement in
person. A slave woman was appointed to watch
over the infant, for whose safety she was made
answerable with her life, until nature had done its
work and the female became attached to her off-
spring.

Bobette, as the nigger woman was called, had
given birth to a strange article, which promised
to become very valuable later on. A métisse with
two green eyes had brought three thousand five
hundred livres at auction in Pointe-à-Pitre. True,
she had been a métisse *à talents*, but there was no
reason why this one should not acquire talents,
M. Mortier himself would see to that. Unfor-

tunately, little Rosalie could not be separated
from her mother, because whenever it was at-
tempted she contracted infections of the mouth,
eyes, and abdomen, and her listless look gave
grounds for fear of consumption. The niggers
said the umbilical cord had been badly cut and
that nothing could be done about it. M. Mortier
resigned himself and had Bobette watched closely
for fear that she damage the child, as mothers
often did with children of the *pariade*. From time
to time he had the child brought to the "château,"
where she was oiled, bathed, and prettied in every
way, so as to make her special status clear to
everyone. But despite the welts on her body, for
which Bobette sometimes paid with welts on her
own, the child apparently had no desire to live
at the big house. No sooner was she cleaned and
polished than she wallowed screaming and squeal-
ing in the dust, with the result that she returned
to the nigger huts exactly as she had left them.
One day when she was almost four, Polycarpe, the
mulatto overseer, reported that he had seen her
plaster her face with black muck from a brook
and admire her reflection in the water. Patience
would be needed, he told M. Mortier, for obvi-
ously the cord was still attached to her umbilicus;

however, he concluded with a smile, there was no
need for the master to worry, for mulattoes always lose their cord in the end.

Bobette's running away was no great blow to
M. Mortier, it was a relief, a saving. The poor
thing had never got used to her new life. In less
than four years this young girl, hardly more than
a child, had turned into one of those ghastly old
hags, the plague of the plantations, who bring in
little more than the cost of their daily mash. Indeed, Christian charity alone had prevented M.
Mortier from "disposing" of her, as some of the
planters, known for their brutality, would have
done. The child was entrusted to the care of a
neighbor woman, and for several weeks M. Mortier had her discreetly watched. According to
Polycarpe, the overseer of the quarter, the little
girl was well behaved but had an absent, thoughtful look that boded no good. In disregard of his
warning, M. Mortier decided to make a present
of the child to his daughter Xavière, who was the
same age as Rosalie and, he felt sure, would be
sufficiently touched by her story as to make a pet
of her. Xavière was a gentle, sweet-natured child;
there was no danger of her harming so precious
an object. The only trouble was Rosalie's un-

fortunate stammer, which had come over her soon
after her mother's departure. According to Polycarpe, who was suspicious of everything, the little
girl did not stammer when she sang; conse-
quently, it could only be a sign of malice, her way
of running away like her mother. M. Mortier
ordered an incision to be made under her tongue
with a razor. The little girl did not seem to suffer.
A trickle of blood flowed from between her lips,
which were turned down at the corners, giving her
the expression of a pike. The cut was treated with
arnica, and she went right on stammering. M.
Mortier took her by the hand and led her to Man
Loulouze, the governess. "Wash your devil," Man
Loulouze commanded; the child sat down calmly
in the basin and soaped the little pink devil between her thighs just as in former days she had
soaped her horny feet and the hair that straggled
over her shoulders, just as she had rubbed her
teeth with ashes and polished them with lemon
wood. Man Loulouze sniffed her all over and
finally made her announcement: The nigger smell
was gone. Then she kissed her on both cheeks and
looking her straight in the eye said severely:

"If you haven't got a mother, you must let
your grandmother nurse you. . . ."

M. Mortier had her dressed in white organdy (though her feet were left bare in accordance with the custom) and took her to Xavière, who, amazed at her eyes, each of a different color, asked her if it was true that people called her Two-Souls. Xavière's four little slave girls burst out laughing. Pleased with her reception, M. Mortier slipped out into the corridor. But through the jalousies in the doorway he looked on, not without emotion, at the touching scene inside. Standing in the middle of the drawing room with a dreamy absent look, Rosalie stammered calmly: "Y-yes, that's w-what they c-call me." Xavière frowned and said testily: "You must say 'yes, mistress.'" And Nini, the quadroon, said: "Mistress, give her a cooling." The malicious Fifine chimed in: "Yes, mistress, a good one." And to M. Mortier's dismay his gentle Xavière encouraged the preparations. The strange little métisse folded her skirt back neatly and lay down on her belly. Each of the four slave girls took hold of a wrist or an ankle. The young mistress picked up a cunning little bone-handled whip and, grimacing like an overseer, raised it above her head.

M. Mortier stifled a cry. For a brief moment he glimpsed the evil that slave brought upon master, both riveted to a chain that bound them more closely than love. But already the playful child, instead of chastising her new slave, caressed her neck with the whip and burst out laughing, as did the other little girls. Then she lifted Rosalie up with her own hands and said with a smile: "I'm not like my sister, Adelaide, I never play with the whip. But you must say 'mistress' to me, or papa will be displeased and my sister will make fun of me. Now you understand; you will call me 'mistress,' won't you?"

The little slave nodded obediently and Xavière changed the subject: "And now tell me, have you really got two souls?"

"Keppe, keppe." Striking her palate with the back of her tongue, she made the sound with which black women express their indignation: "Keppe, keppe. Is this what Man Bobette wanted of me? Is it?"

And yet she went about her business in the big house, affable to all, indifferent to all, carefully preserving the insipid mask she had laid on her face. Three weeks of "finishing" had transformed her. Bathed, rested, well fed, bled just a little for the good of her complexion, washed in cassia and

tamarind, massaged with castor oil, which loosens
the joints, she was a far cry from the frightening
animal with a trickle of blood at the corners of
her mouth that had been admitted to the ark
three weeks before. Her airy, graceful neck
formed a right angle with her Egyptian shoulders, and she held her slender arms at her sides
like an articulated wax doll. All in all, she was
quite the drawing-room shepherdess. But there
was a chilling absence in her eyes; they seemed to
shimmer with a mineral life of their own, like the
suspended glass globes in Mme. Mortier's room,
which revolved slowly from morning to night. Behind those eyes, deep in her doll-like head, all
sorts of new thoughts darted about like crabs.
Never before had she felt so close to Man Bobette's secret. And as she came and went in the
big house, learning proper manners, learning how
to smile and curtsy, mysterious phrases crossed
her mind like shooting stars. Sometimes in the
kitchen, in the dining room, or in Mademoiselle
Xavière's room, she would hear a familiar voice
murmuring: "Land of white men, land of madness." Then she would quickly lower her eyelids,
the crabs darted their claws into her head, and
Man Bobette spoke words of warning: "Careful.

The man who knows you is a beast that kills."
And if she complained, putting the blame for the
life she was leading on her mother, Man Bobette
silenced her with the retort: "When a fly dies in a
wound, that is where it was meant to die." And
accepting her mother's judgment, Two-Souls
would shut her eyes still tighter. But at other
times she would stiffen her neck with rage and let
the crabs fly at Man Bobette, or thrust out her
belly and hurl the crabs at the big house, brandish
torches, cutlasses, and phials of poison, and find
herself in the end nailed to the post at the en-
trance to the nigger village. And the harsh voice
of Man Bobette murmured in consolation: "When
you know that an arrow won't miss you, just
thrust out your belly to receive it squarely."

Her duties were nothing compared to work in
the fields. When the bell rang, she gave herself a
good wash to chase away the nigger smell. After
dressing daintily, she would help the girls with
kinky hair to make their heads presentable. Then
they all went to the kitchen, where she would have
a mango or a custard for breakfast. Then they
hurried to their mistress's room, where the shut-
ters were still closed, and watched for her to wake
up, each sitting motionless in a corner, holding

her breath, while the pink and blond shape reposed under her muslin dome. Two-Souls learned to wash her little mistress and do her hair, and though she sometimes exasperated her with her stammering, earning a tap of the forefinger across her lips, she gradually became her favorite, her pet, eating sherbet with her, scratching the soles of her feet at siesta time, listening to her stories and responding with a bit of kitchen gossip or a little song in patois, which the mistress learned eagerly, as though, moved by a love intermingled with contempt that had come to her with her wet nurse's milk, she longed in some secret recess of her heart to be a little savage herself. Mistress Xavière was so white that she seemed made of wax, and Man Loulouze whispered that she would not live long. She had spells of dizziness and vomiting; she never went out in the sun without a parasol, a straw hat, and a lace veil that hung down over her shoulders. A thorn, a cross word from her mother, a mere nothing would make her bury her head in her pillow and cry for hours. But she never complained, she never raised her voice, not even when M. Hubert or Mlle. Adelaide hurt one of her pets. She had no taste at all for belly-wallowing like young M.

Hubert, nor for riding, like Mlle. Adelaide, in a little carriage drawn by eight pickaninnies harnessed like horses. She preferred her dolls, her macaw, her music box with its prickly cylinders, which played "Le Troubadour" and "Le Carnaval de Venise." She never spoke of skinning you alive or of cleaning the rotten meat off your bones, or of teaching you to sleep for three months on your elbows, with your bottom in the air. But some of her little jokes were not at all to Two-Souls' liking. For instance, when one of her pets had displeased her, she would say: "I shall sell you to M. Chaperon." This Chaperon was a planter who had shut up one of his slaves in a hot oven, and the masters had got into the habit of threatening their slaves with this bogeyman. Two-Souls knew that Mlle. Xavière had no intention of selling any of her pets to M. Chaperon. But when she heard these words, spoken lightly, in a tone both gentle and sad, she hated Mlle. Xavière more than all the other whites in the big house. Sometimes she told herself that her mistress had drunk from the madwoman's gourd, and sometimes she smilingly remembered one of Man Bobette's sayings: "Some people talk so much they can't even feel their ass without saying, It's not mine." But most often, as she considered Mlle. Xavière's pale and gently sad features, she murmured to herself with secret rage: "Land of white women, land of lies."

Often Mlle. Xavière kept Two-Souls with her for the night. A mat would be tossed on the floor for her to sleep on. In long conversations in the darkness, Two-Souls was initiated into the world of the whites and mulattoes. She knew she was being discreetly watched, on the supposition that she might somehow be in communication with her mother. Some of the mulattoes, especially Man Loulouze, even insinuated that she was the runaways' accomplice. Mlle. Xavière also thought a good deal about runaway niggers and kept bringing up the subject. They were different from other people, she thought; they had made a pact with the devil and his likeness was stamped on them somewhere. She couldn't believe that Two-Souls had never seen anything of the kind on her mother. One proof of their pact with the devil, she often said, was their insensibility to torture. Didn't Two-Souls know that niggers didn't feel pain as white people do?

"Everybody knows that, mistress," said Two-Souls in a fright.

But runaway niggers, Mademoiselle went on in her sweet gentle voice, didn't seem to feel anything at all. There was sorcery behind it, no other explanation was possible. Whatever you did to them, they just smiled or calmly insulted you, as though you weren't worthy of their anger. Her father, too, she went on with a look of alarm, was sure the devil had a hand in it. He had seen niggers put to the torture of the ants, the sack, the barrel, the garrote, the ladder, the hammock, the swing, and the wax; he had seen melted lard poured over them and gunpowder stuffed in their openings; he had seen them buried alive with and without quicklime, smoked and crucified; and as far as he could make out, it hadn't done a bit of good: still the same smile on their accursed lips, the same insolent faraway look, as if you didn't really exist. . . .

Despite her fear, Two-Souls, who remembered the Bambara woman, was secretly filled with joy, sorrow, and infinite tenderness. She couldn't help asking:

"Don't red ants hurt them either, mistress?"

"Why red ants?" asked Mlle. Xavière.

"Because," said Two-Souls, "that's what I like best." Which was her childlike way of saying that it was what she feared more than anything else in the world.

"Me," Mlle. Xavière confided, "it's having all my teeth pulled, one by one, the way M. Chaperon does. My teeth are so sensitive that I'd die, even if I were a nigger. . . ."

And then she gave a charming yawn, covering her mouth with her hand as the people in the big house did. Two-Souls slipped under the netting and expertly scratched the soles of her feet with her fine fingernails. Sometimes it took a song to put Mlle. Xavière to sleep, sometimes a murmur, sometimes silence. She always wanted the same song, the cane-cutters' song of Zulma, perhaps because of its plaintive tune, which harmonized with the weary movements of her heart.

> Kill me but give me my Zulma
> Give me back my Zulma
> For to live without her
> I haven't the strength

When Mademoiselle had fallen asleep, Two-Souls arose quietly and went to the window. Through the mosquito screen she could see the outline of the mountain in the bright night. She saw fires on the heights. They were glowworms dangling from a nearby branch or stars over the mountain peaks, but the child liked to think they were the runaways' campfires, and she dreamed of Bobette, the heroic black woman. She dreamed of her for hours, punctuating her reverie with a reproachful "keppe, keppe," addressed to her mother, who was making her wait so long: How many days, how many weeks had already passed? At every sound, the least cracking of a twig, her heart stopped beating: Had the time come? And then orange mists trailed through the sky and the child lay down again on her mat beside her mistress, making feebler and feebler "keppe keppes" at the back of her throat, until at last, still shaken with indignation, she fell asleep.

At about this time a certain Carrousel ran off to the woods and came back two months later of his own free will, crying his heart out. The poor devil wanted to expiate his crime. He tore his sunken cheeks with his nails and licked the sole of M. Mortier's boot. He said the devil had taken hold of him and dragged him to the woods with a long invisible rope. Such sorcery was not unusual on the plantations. His masters believed the poor freshwater nigger and poured tabasco sauce on his wounds to make him remember them. Then they put an iron muzzle on him and an iron collar, surmounted by an enormous St. Andrew's cross, and sent him back to the fields without delay. He walked as though in a procession. The arms of his cross teetered, dragging him down in a slow, solemn fall. His muzzle was taken off once a day at feeding time. Then he murmured an Our Father and said a few words, always harking back to his odyssey in the woods. One day he said he had seen black Bobette high up on La Soufrière, with a group of saltwater niggers. She had grown hair, she seemed surprisingly young, she slept with a big Arada, and had just given birth to a child, as pretty and black as a coco plum.

Inhabited by a strange fever, the little girl began to dream. Every night as she looked at the mountain, it seemed to her that she was falling into the sky like a dead fish. Terror-stricken, she said to herself: "So this is how it is. Can it really be like this?" And by a strange quirk of the soul she forced herself to be more obedient than ever, to make herself useful from morning to night, to be the sweetest little pet in the world. She developed a taste for it; all at once she discovered an unsuspected pleasure in making a show of servil-

ity. At first this flowering of virtue was thought
alarming but soon all suspicion was disarmed.
Man Loulouze took her to her bosom, Mlle.
Xavière entrusted her macaw to her care, and M.
Mortier, now fully confident, had her given les-
sons in sewing, French, the Indian harp, and
above all singing, for, so he said, she sang like a
young dove. But one fine day, without prompting
from her head, her hands poured fresh manioc
juice into the chickens' feeding trough, and they
all expired in agony. She wondered how she could
communicate this glorious exploit to her mother,
who was so far away, on the heights of La Soufrière; then she decided there was no need to tell
her mother, for she had done it all by herself, for
her own satisfaction. And anyway, Man Bobette
could die as far as she was concerned, die like the
chickens, with rigid legs and bloodshot eyes and
her black mouth open like a funnel: "Bon voyage,"
Two-Souls would say. "Bon voyage, ma chère."
She looked for another opportunity to be *wicked*,
something even more delicious, something that
would hit humans, black, yellow, or white regardless. She was so full of her new feelings that she
took pleasure in the humiliations encountered in
the corridors of the mansion: They were like stones

piling up in her heart, they would give her strength when the time came. . . .

Then she began to worry about *changing*. She feared it and wanted it, but most of the time she was desperately afraid. Suppose she changed into something terrifying, a dog, for instance, as certain wicked people were said to do. And the little girl wondered which she would prefer, to turn into a dog that looked like a dog, or a dog in human form, like that emaciated nigger, all skin and bone, she had seen one day when Mlle. Xavière had taken her to visit some neighbors at Bas-Carbet; that old nigger, stark naked in his kennel, with his eyes closed and an iron collar on his neck. She thought and thought, but she could not decide which she preferred, or which she dreaded more. She began to bark in her dreams, and her mistress sent her to sleep in the outhouse with the other servants. Soon they too complained, and a mat was laid for her in the ruined old sugar mill behind the big house. There she was all alone and glad of it. Her only company was the macaw, who perched tilt-headed on a bar and croaked in his sleep. Sometimes his croaking troubled her, she went over to him, tilting her head as he did, and said in a tone of gentle exasperation: "What am I to do with you? To beat you wouldn't be enough, and to kill you would be too much." She took the bird in her arms, rocked him, hummed a kind of lullaby, and put him back on his bar, which his claws gripped of their own accord. Then she stood bolt upright in the middle of the room, slowly pivoting her head on her neck for hours as the darkness deepened and invaded her heart, subtly bidding her to *change*. . . .

According to an oral tradition, still living on the Côte-sous-le-Vent, not far from the peaks of Deshaies, Bayangumay's little girl was about eleven when she turned into a zombie. At that time, say the old Creole storytellers, the black people were pursued by an evil spirit; a man would go to bed in his right mind and when he woke up he would be a dog, a toad, or a zombie, just as nowadays you might wake up with white hairs. No one was surprised when it happened, the people would say: oh. Nothing more, just oh. At that time there were all sorts of Shadows on the sugar islands: dead blacks revived by magic, living blacks who moved into the bodies of animals, and many many more whose souls had gone off no one knew where. These last were commonly known as zombies. They worked like oxen, and when their work was done they stood still, like oxen. Zombies were simply humans whose souls had deserted them; they were still alive, but the soul was gone.

These years are obscure and their chronicle uncertain. It is known, however, that the child was sold and delivered at Basse-Terre on February 8, 1784. In the last months of her stay at the du Parc plantation she seems to have worked in the fields with the black cattle. The new masters branded her on the shoulder and sent her to the cane fields. They thought they had bought a body with a soul attached, but when they heard her laugh they spread their ten fingers and unloaded her at another slave market. It was the same with the masters who followed; they heard her laugh and spread their ten fingers. And like cattle raisers, they all left their initials on her body. She became so wild that men were able to possess her only by force or by surprise. Yet in spite of her dead, glassy eyes and the nasal voice characteristic of the spirits of the dead, she grew so beautiful that her claws did not stop them. One day, she put her own mark on her shoulders, in a manner of speaking. It was the dry season, she was digging a yam trench not far from the road from Le Gosier to Morne-à-l'Eau. The master was hard, the herd stark naked except for the young mothers, who wore a few rags around their waists. The overseers' whips were singing. A poor white stopped by the roadside and said in the voice they have for saying that kind of thing: "*Ki nom a ou ti fi?*" Which means: "What is your name, little girl?" She straightened up, leaned on her hoe, and laughed in the manner of those who are absent, floating on the waters of perdition. Then in a monotone shot through with the same laugh, she uttered the words that were to cling to her throughout her brief eternity:

"By your leave, master: My name is Solitude."

4

THE CHEVALIER DE DANGEAU was a tall, slender, beribboned man with a narrow beaklike nose, a perpetual smile, and a look of weariness in his large restless eyes. He had come late to the islands, after a brief period of service in North America under the Marquis de Lafayette. Though he fancied himself from the first as a philosopher in the powdered manner of the day, he soon realized that he had neither the fortune nor the rank to keep pace with his wit, and hid his preoccupations behind gracious manners and a smile that disclosed the finest teeth imaginable. In the course of time, however, he came into fashion, obtained official appointments and concessions of land, and recovered his taste for philosophy. By then the high society of the island had

taken it up. The conversation in the drawing
rooms revolved about *man* and his intrinsic vir-
tues. Masonic lodges were founded, where en-
lightened spirits discussed the delta and the tetra-
gram, the architecture of the heavens, and the
possibility of granting mulattoes the right to
wear shoes. The chevalier renamed his slave ship
La Nouvelle Héloïse. His mansion, at the center
of a park enclosed in high walls, was The Temple
of Delights. Each week a select group gathered
there. Often their conversation turned to the abbé
Raynal's celebrated book on the East and West Indian trade, certain passages in which filled them
with consternation and moved them to tears. The
chevalier dreamed of an ideal slave trade, more
chary of human suffering. But alas, he concluded
with a weary smile, it makes so little difference
here below whether one does good or evil. He
often told anecdotes about M. Voltaire, whom he
had known well during his years in Paris. The
illustrious old man, it was said, had invested
heavily in *La Nouvelle Héloïse*. The chevalier's
association with the eminent philosopher cast an
aura of greatness and wisdom over his small talk.

These conversations took place in the presence
of ten or a dozen slaves of both sexes, mentioned

by many travelers among the greatest marvels and curiosities of the islands. The chevalier instructed them according to the precepts of his master Jean-Jacques. He had selected them with care: They must be young, gifted in mind and heart, and their features must be at once regular and grave. Dressed in the finest silks, as resplendent as idols, these slaves participated in all the pleasures of the drawing room and boudoir. They spoke like philosophers, sang like angels, and played all the fashionable instruments, including the French horn.

The chevalier de Dangeau bought the métisse Solitude on August 23, 1787, at an auction in Pointe-à-Pitre. He had come to purchase a violinist, a talented young lady, who was said to have been trained at the slave school in New Orleans. When he arrived, the violinist was standing on the main platform. At her feet the rising bids rang out like applause. She was dressed in pink taffeta, her long black cheeks were blue with powder, but the chevalier found her a little too fat for his taste. Feeling vaguely out of sorts, he wandered about the enormous warehouse, piled high with goods and crowded with slaves, awaiting their fate in silent immobility. Snatches of violin music drifted in, and from time to time he caught a heartbreaking phrase. In one corner a young girl with a listless look was sitting, her head propped on one hand, on a case of wine, guarded by a local militiaman. She was dressed in a bulky jute sack with three holes in it; her feet were bare and her hair disheveled. People stepped up to question her: "Are you a good girl?—Can you launder?—Can you work in the garden?—Can you iron?—Why are they selling you?—Mightn't you be a runaway?" She answered sullenly, and the prospective buyer said: "Open your mouth so I can hear you, you imbecile." As a customer was lifting her chin by force to investigate the state of her teeth, the chevalier saw she had two transparent eyes of different colors in a face of silk and ashes, the sibylline face of a dead child. . . .

The bidding rose to four hundred francs. Cold and impassive, she stood leaning against a piece of furniture. With a gesture in the direction of the last bidder, the auctioneer said to her: "All right, there's your new master." She raised her eyes to the chevalier and went over to him, still with the same listless air. At the chevalier's bidding, her body was drenched in musk and oint-

ments, creams and perfumes. She was fitted out
with bracelets and anklets, with Creole necklaces
and strings of gold and silver ornaments, with
coral and garnet earrings. This costume, known
at the time as *la pimpante*, was topped off by a
bright yellow madras which gave her the absent
exotic look of a parrot. The chevalier was moved
by her air of strange melancholy. He examined
her glassy eyes, which seemed sightless, indifferent to what was going on around her. Just then
she laughed. The woman who had dressed her and
was contemplating her work shuddered and
passed a trembling hand over her flat face, as
though to dispel a vision. Next day the chevalier
saw that his drawing-room slaves were gazing at
the new girl with bewildered sadness, and guiding
her steps as though she were blind. They seemed
to think she was "different," essentially different,
and some said she had no soul. The chevalier was
unfamiliar with this ailment, and his guests
smiled as they contemplated the grave, docile
child. But after the first surprise, the first flush
of novelty, all felt puzzingly frustrated. The
child's kisses and caresses, even her beauty,
seemed to be made of nothing. She reminded one
of a mechanical toy, one of those dancing dolls

that twist and turn on a few tinkling notes, then suddenly stop still when the spring is unwound. She did everything she was told, as eager to carry out orders as a well-trained dog; but if you turned away for a moment, she would lapse into immobility, and when you looked back she had the vacant gaze of a sleepwalker. She began to scream at night, because of something or other she had heard in the smoking room. Some harmless joke no doubt had worked darkly on her mind. In her nightmare, always the same, she saw herself changed into a sugar statue, which the Frenchmen of France were slowly eating far far away at the other end of the world, first breaking off her fingers, so thin and long that they seemed unreal. The chevalier took pity on her and had her transferred to the kitchen, where for several years she led the peaceful life of a zombie. Her laughter subsided into a faint, fleeting smile. With the peace that had come over her, she became so docile that the prayers of all those about her were hers to command. The chevalier saw to it that no one took advantage of her helplessness. She was seldom brought to the drawing room, only on musical evenings because of her exquisite voice. All agreed that there wasn't a young lady on the is-

land who could sing the songs of the day so gracefully. Inclining her head, curving her neck like a
swan, she sang:

> Paris is such a charming place
> Who'd ever leave it except for paradise?

And so life went on until the Revolution came
to the island. On May 7, 1795, the troops of the
Convention landed at Grande-Terre de Guadeloupe, where they published the decree abolishing
slavery; on May 12, reinforced by slaves encountered on the way, they entered the suburbs of
Pointe-à-Pitre. The chevalier de Dangeau took a
horse, two pistols, and a sword, and joined the
royalists and English, who were camped on the
other side of the Salée River, on Guadeloupe
proper. Some of his slaves wanted to go with him,
but the chevalier repulsed them violently, saying
they were worse than groveling dogs. He himself,
he explained, was going back to the camp into
which he had been born, but his heart was with the
soldiers of freedom. At the last moment he
stopped to take leave of Solitude and murmured
with infinite sadness: "And you, poor zombie,
who will deliver you from your chains?" "What
chains, Seigneur?" she asked with a smile.

5

THE SLAVES from the burned-out plantations
took refuge on a strip of marshland between the
harbor and the Salée River. They built huts of
anything they could find: planks, branches,
tarred canvas, barrels sawed in two. The fugitives
moved like ships on the sea, each with its own
compass, its own itinerary, each propelled by the
sails of its own fancy. Solitude soon discovered
that there was no room for a zombie in this new
world they called the Republic. She did her best
to imitate the movements of life, but floods of
water kept flowing from her eyes. People wondered where so much water could come from and
made her drink, for fear she would be reduced to
a handful of dust. Some called her Rainbow, because of the smile that filtered through her tears.

She herself was surprised; dipping her fingertips in the dew, she would examine them with interest. Then the waters ebbed; for a few days there was still a trickle, and then only the soft washed stones of her eyes.

She woke up with this group or that group, shadows old and new. After pouring a bit of water on their faces, they would dress in the colors of the day, blue madras, white blouse, spreading crimson skirt. Then they would go to the square by the port, to eat fritters and fish cakes and coconut creams and look on as the heads of the white men fell. Solitude never went too near the guillotine because of the foul sludge around it. Every day fresh earth was thrown over the blood, but the lower layers worked their way upward, and pink splotches appeared between the bare black feet of the onlookers. It was said that when the blacks of Saint-Domingue saw the first head fall, they had rushed at the machine and torn it to pieces. But those of Guadeloupe had soon got used to the new entertainment: They came and went at all hours, ate, drank, and laughed, savored the sweet air of freedom, and blinked sagely at the sun as they watched white men cutting white men's heads off. It was just like France,

they were told; and in the taverns French soldiers
would show them books bound in aristocrat-hide.
In the afternoon when the heads had rolled, when
the drums and brass bands had died down, black
women swarmed through the town, filling the air
with their songs and laughter. Solitude let herself drift along with the stream. For hours on end
they would watch the soldiers drilling on the
charred squares of Pointe-à-Pitre. Field niggers
with gray feet, bare from the waist up except for
their shoulder straps, marched back and forth
under the orders of mounted mulattoes with lofty
plumes. Recognizing companions of servitude,
the onlookers would call out to them or stand up
on tiptoe and throw them kisses as though releas-
ing carrier pigeons. Those who had no friends
among the troops would roll on to Fort de la
Victoire, where the expeditionary force, the
eighth regiment of Pyrenees chasseurs, was quar-
tered. The gates were open, the visitors could
count on a friendly reception in the courtyard,
the white men's faces were barely veiled with
irony. Quite a few of the freshwater Negresses
conceived *chapé* children, children who would
escape (*échapper*) the curse of being black.
These women looked on the events as a sign from

100

God, an assurance that He had pardoned the black race and was going to save it. Already some of them were going about with enlarged bellies, laden with messianic promise. Their eyes shone so intensely that Solitude was dazzled and averted her head. Sometimes, inexplicably, she felt a pang in her side, a kind of soul pain. Then with a bewildered look she held out her arms and tried to attach herself to a different group, to a more helpful wave. . . .

One day on the Place de la Sartine, Solitude noticed that the crowd was not as dense as usual. There was a mysterious tension in the air. No one was singing or dancing the farandole. Suddenly the National Guard surrounded the square. Behind the black heads the cockades and bayonets of the soldiers of the Republic appeared. A groan shook the crowd at the sight of the tumbrel that creaked and rattled as it entered the square from rue Frébault: In it was seated a little field nigger, wide-eyed with astonishment. Solitude's two arms went out, but there was no wave to attach herself to, no current to follow. The people around her seemed panic-stricken, like flies caught in a jar. For a moment the band covered the clamor of the crowd, and out of the corner of her eye Solitude saw the little field nigger's head detach itself from the guillotine and tumble across the sky. She dropped her arms and stood motionless in the middle of the square, waiting for heaven or earth or people to give her body a new direction. Three black women passed, holding one another by the hand. Their rustling skirts bulged, giving them the look of big blue flies. Solitude grabbed hold of one of them and felt herself being lifted into the air. When after a long moment she opened her eyes, the three black women were lying on the ground embracing, seeking refuge in one another. Crawling on her hands and knees, Solitude thrust her head into a bundle of quivering flesh. Then she heard a man's voice, saying in the French of France: "Look here, *citoyennes,* try to be reasonable. . . ."

A black woman moaned: "Liberty shouldn't have done that to us. . . ."

"I agree with you," said the man in a gruff, mournful voice, marked with disillusionment, "but don't try to get away from her, her legs are longer than yours. . . ."

Raising her head, Solitude saw that the man's voice belonged to an old soldier of the eighth Pyrenees regiment. With the sharp point of his bayonet, he negligently grazed the black women on the ground. Not far away a group of blacks had been lined up; their arms were tied behind their backs, and they were strung together by a long rope knotted around each neck—like slaves being dragged to an auction. A detachment of black National Guards were standing off to one side, their guns leveled at the silent file. Their shifting eyes seemed to see no one. Solitude thrust out her neck and the knot closed under her chin with the surprising gentleness of a caress.

The order to march was given. The rope tensed with a musical twang and once again, but more deeply, Solitude felt that the rope around her neck was a bond between her and her kind. Her lips moved in a faint smile. . . .

Led by two grenadiers, the roped blacks made their way to a plantation at Baie-Mahaut on the Côte-sous-le-Vent, where some fifty "agricultural workers" were already at work under the surveillance of a detachment of National Guards. The regimen was mild; the whips were decorated with tricolor ribbons, and their use was regulated by a strict scale of offenses and not, as formerly, by the whim of the planters. And the new order wasn't really slavery as the workers had feared during

their long march: they were still "citizens," and
they worked to the strains of the new Marseil-
laise, written by a certain Dosse of Matouba:

Allons enfants de la Guinée,
Le jour de travail est arrivé,
Ah, telle est notre destinée,
Au jardin avant soleil levé,
C'est ainsi que la loi ordonne.
Soumettons-nous à son décret,
Travaillons sans aucun regret
Pour mériter ce qu'on nous donne.
A la houe, citoyens, formez vos bataillons
Fouillons avec ardeur, faisons de bons sillons.

Rise, children of Guinea,
The day of labor is at hand.
Ah, such is our destiny:
To the garden before sunrise,
For that is the law.
Let us submit to its decree,
Let us work without regret
To deserve what is given us,
To the hoe, citizens, drawn up your battalions.
Let us dig with a will and make good furrows.

Solitude felt almost calm; the orders and pun-
ishments reassured her. After a day in the fields,

she would cook a potful of roots. Sitting on a
stone in front of her cabin of branches, she would
dip her hand into the pot and then into her mouth,
as though in a dream. Rain or shine, she would sit
there until late into the night. Her companions
had their misgivings: What was she looking at
through her lowered lashes? But since the children
liked her and seemed to bask in her gaze, she was
left unmolested on her stone.

Most often she saw nothing but merely floated
in space, now and then picking a bit of food out
of her pot. But sometimes, when no one suspected
it, she raised her lashes a little and watched the
woman who lived in the next hut. Her name was
Frosiane Mabolo, but people also called her
Frosiane Stinking Bandage, because of the filthy
rag she tied around the festering wound on her
leg. A Congo both on her father's and mother's
side, she was about thirty. Her back had been
branded by three successive owners. She was a true
field animal, with feet devoured by chigoes and
big thick hands. But her skin was admirable, a
deep, soft blue-black, which attracted the light
like a magnet and made it revolve around her like
a sort of halo. And then there was her laugh,
which sometimes reminded Solitude of Man Bobette. Frosiane would lean back and look up at the

sky and laugh. The sound seemed to rise from the
bottom of a well, a real black woman's laugh. When
she saw that skin and heard that laugh, Solitude
smiled to herself behind her half-closed eyelids.

Frosiane knew it, but didn't seem to mind. She
even let Solitude follow her at a distance like a
timid dog. She called her "my shadow." But one
evening as Solitude was sitting on her stone, Frosiane flew into a rage and said:

"Why are you laughing? I want to know."

"I'm not laughing," said Solitude.

"Shadow, you're lying; you're lying like a
yellow dog."

Solitude was frightened. "No, no," she protested.

For a moment Frosiane seemed to be thinking;
then with the same feverish rage as before:

"Why wouldn't you laugh? Tell me that! Why
wouldn't a thing like you laugh once in a while?
Haven't you got a mouth and teeth? That's reason enough to laugh, take it from me, Frosiane:
just having a mouth and teeth."

"Reason enough," Solitude murmured. "Reason enough, reason enough . . ."

A few nights later runaway blacks attacked the
national workshop at La Baie-Mahaut. Frosiane

106

was monologuing to her shadow, who understood nothing, but nodded now and then. Suddenly cries were heard from the hilltop, from the direction of the master's house, which had been occupied by the manager, the overseers, and the National Guards. Shots rang out, cries were heard, and then the whole hill was in flames.

A few of the workers ran off into the night, brandishing their machetes. But when they reached the hilltop, it was all over: The rebels were removing the last stitches of clothing from the black corpses of the National Guards, the yellow corpses of the overseers, and the white corpse of the manager. The black women surrounded the assailants, kissing their weapons, kissing their knees, kissing their blood-stained hands. Many of the women were crying out of mad, protuberant eyes. But not a word escaped from their lips, not a moan, not a cry. Solitude had followed her friend, anxiously tugging at her sleeve, like a dog reminding his master of his existence. In the light of the flames the runaways enlisted those who wanted to join their ranks. Almost all the blacks stepped forward. When she saw the column vanishing into the darkness, Solitude felt a fire in her chest, and started running with all her might. But the men of the rear guard spread their arms and one of them said coldly: "What do you want with us, you yellow shit?"

Only the mulatto citizens were left, six of them, and a few women who were too old and decrepit, or too heavily pregnant, and with too many children on their hands. As the column of rebels made their way upward to the woods, the pitiful remnant started for Pointe-à-Pitre to put themselves in the hands of the authorities. They loaded as much of the National Guards, the overseers, and the manager as they could find into a hand cart and took it along. But seized with fright as they approached the Salée River, they abandoned the cart and scattered. Left to herself, Solitude sat down on the ground, leaning on one of the cart wheels. Her tongue dangled from her open mouth and she whimpered like an animal. Faint lights could be seen in the distance, behind the masts in the harbor. . . .

6

Leaving Pointe-à-Pitre, the guillotine haunted
the countryside. It climbed the steep, desolate hills
in pursuit of citizens who did not understand their
new duties. Many took refuge from liberty, equal-
ity, and fraternity in the deep dark woods, where
they rested from their new-style torments. Special
detachments haunted them day and night. Nigger
dogs, the big spotted mastiffs of former days, were
no longer available; they had been exterminated
in the first days of Abolition. Their work was done
by republican blacks, and most efficiently thanks
to the color of their skins and their secret ties with
the runaways. First the organized bands, then the
isolated groups were gradually wiped out.

Only the runaway camp by the Goyave River,
the last bastion of the saltwater blacks of Guade-

loupe, remained. Their commander was one Sanga, a Mandingo who had been captured by Victor Hugues's corsairs from a Spanish slave ship off the Virgin Islands. Always eager to replenish the coffers of the Republic, Hugues had issued instructions that such "liberated" slaves were to be quietly taken to the free ports of the Dutch islands. What with the perils of the crossing and the depletion of the African coasts, the price of black ivory was at its highest. But some of the captains, who had not forgotten the year II of the Revolution, dropped their cargo on the shores of Guadeloupe, which were undoubtedly more hospitable, yes, undoubtedly. These liberated Africans were known as nigger castaways. Uncomprehending, they wandered through the chaos of a mysterious civil war, obediently following anyone who showed them an enemy. Successively Sanga was thrown into battle against the English, the soldiers of the Republic, the poor whites and the *ci-devant* aristocrats, and against patriots of all shades, blacks and sacatras, mulattoes, quadroons, and even those mysterious Kalmanquious, whose skin and eyes, it was said on the sugar islands, were clouded by a single drop of black blood. One day, after fighting everyone there was to fight, the castaway sat down and coldly considered the facts. His thoughts culminated in a kind of illumination. A somber ecstasy in his eyes, but lips radiant with joy, he made his way to the runaways by the Goyave and quickly became their leader, chosen by the Gods of Africa. His doctrine had the simplicity of revelation. All blacks, he said, have the same father and the same mother; all spring from a common stock, as do the agoutis, the manfesnils, and other beasts and birds. If some among them had forgotten this, it was because of invisible eggs that the white men had laid in their heads unbeknownst to them. As for him, he concluded with a bitter laugh—as for him, Sanga, scion of the land of Bornu, he would tolerate only those who had crushed the eggs the white men had laid in their heads and whose only thoughts were of Africa—beautiful black thoughts which knew no treason. . . .

The camp was set up on a plateau, halfway up the mountain. There, in the midst of an ageless forest, the runaways had cleared ground, built huts, and planted garden crops. Sanga governed them with an iron hand, as though he were in the heart of his native Bornu. Several times his men had repulsed the attacks of General Desfourneaux, whose mission it was to hunt all those who rejected the "beneficent laws of the great nation." Look-outs were posted on the banks of the Goyave, which separated the rebels from the hostile world. At the slightest alarm, at the first sign of "rat hunters," the conch horns wailed. The women and children scrambled up the mountain, while the men took up their positions on the borders of Little Guinea, as they called their small enclave in the white man's country. Sanga owed his pres-tige to a book which he displayed to the peasants. That one book, he said, contained the entire doc-trine—a ruse by which he appropriated the magic of the masters. When General Desfourneaux finally destroyed the camp, a small vellum-bound volume was found among the tattered corpses. All sorts of African ornaments had been traced on its pages with vegetable inks. The book was *Les Rêveries du Promeneur Solitaire* by Jean-Jacques Rousseau.

One evening in December 1798, a few weeks before the end, a lookout spied a silhouette mov-ing over the flat stones of the Goyave. The man was sitting behind a bush, his gun wedged be-tween his knees. His head was perfectly motionless but his eyes swiveled from side to side over the darkening waters. A human form was jumping from stone to stone with the silent, hesitant application of an insect. Arrived at the middle of the ford, it was outlined for a moment against the waterfall. Then a gust of wind parted the spray, revealing a small yellow woman, tattered and half naked. Her bundle, fastened to a short stick that she carried on her shoulder, bobbed up and down and her shaggy unkempt hair looked like a hen's nest. The man waited until she had set foot on the last stone. Then, leveling his gun, he cried out in a voice hoarse with fear: "Who goes there, woman? Hey!"

She seemed to stagger on her stone. The great rolling globes in her sunken eye sockets were like the unseeing eyes of visitors from the other world, and terror squeezed the man's heart. Then her mouth opened. Confused words came out, a soft, musical stammer, silk rubbing on silk: "B-beg your pardon," she muttered, smiling with emotion. "H-have you seen an old runaway black woman . . . Man Bobette . . . you know . . . from the du Parc plantation . . . you know . . . long long ago, over by Carbet de Capesterre? . . ." A smile brushed across her lips, a

smile veiled with irony, which seemed to address
itself to an ancient presence, a shade, infinitely
near and infinitely inaccessible. "H-have
you? . . ." she began again in confusion. Then
pivoting on the stone, she started back across the
river, reached the singing curtain of the waterfall,
threw out her arms and fell into the waist-deep
water. There she remained as though drunk, silent
and motionless, without so much as turning toward the petrified black man on the bank. An
eddy swelled her skirt and spread it out on the
water, turning her into an aquatic plant that
leaned this way and that as the current shifted.
The man cupped his hand over his mouth and
called out to her in a muffled voice: "Hey, the river
is cold. Hey! Hey . . ." Suddenly leaping out
over the stones, he seized her by the hair and
pulled her up like a dripping fish. She sat shivering in the grass and smiled. Her slender body
exuded a terrifying smell. "Little leaf," he said.
"Little yellow leaf. The mother of men isn't happy
these days." Motioning her to get up, he started
for the camp. From time to time he slackened his
pace to let the little shape catch up. The lookouts
stationed at intervals along the path commented
on the strange woman's smell as they passed. The

man, who could only agree, replied with colorful comparisons. After a while, when she kept silent, he thought he had gone too far, that no human being deserved to be so insulted. He stopped still, casting about for a word of consolation. Then he heard that she was singing inside her mouth, humming very softly. And though she was out of breath her humming was unmistakably joyful. . . .

Soon the path came to an end. The runaways were sitting around a fire which cast a cone of light high into the sky, high above men and mountains. Along the line of huts a few children were moving about amid piles of guns, spears, Carib clubs, and big curved sabers. Here and there tangled lianas hung from the trees. The adults spoke softly, knowingly, and since their eyes were all turned toward the fire, each one of them seemed to be carrying on a long conversation with himself. A group of women came to meet the new arrivals. One of them was a mountainous black woman, with cheeks like hills and arms like rivers, nobly draped in a pagne that hung down to her feet. A bead was affixed to one of her nostrils, an infant slept on her back, held in place by a square of cloth knotted below her breasts. Apparently she was not the baby's mother, for her hair was a gray sponge, her eyebrows were white, and she had no lashes. Her name was Euphrosine Gellanbé, an inversion of her first master's name. The man told her the creature had fallen into the river, and she led her to the fire. But several women left the circle in disgust. One of them cried out in a piercing voice that this mulatto really was yellow shit. Some held their noses, others laughed, and the creature smiled vaguely, looking about her, listening to the talk with an expression of ethereal happiness. Suddenly the old Congo woman cried out in despair: "You apes, don't you remember that smell?" And kneeling at the creature's feet, pointing a finger at her swollen ankles, at her calves grooved with recent shackles, said in a thin, flutelike voice: "*Oh, my children, don't you remember the smell of the rotting pit?*" Great tears flowed down her cheeks. The women prepared hot water, undressed the victim, and laid poultices of soft grass on the wounds made by the rotting irons. The creature submitted passively, without a word, without a sign of embarrassment. The runaways screwed up their eyes to examine her belly and back, traversed by pink welts and older marks that were fading as the skin grew back. The serein set in, the bushes swayed in the breeze, drops fell

here and there, the lianas trembled, the larger
trees seemed on the point of toppling. A blanket
was thrown over her shoulders, and the otherwise
naked creature sat by the fire with legs crossed
and body erect, looking about at this one and that
one with pitiful eyes, which one moment seemed
lifeless and the next radiant, full of a timeless
friendship without beginning or end. All dreaded
to meet her glance and looked down when it came
their way. A young Congo woman handed her a
cassava cake and bending over her stroked her
long damp hair, murmuring in a tone barely
tinged with jealousy: "The poor yellow leaf; you
can see she must have been beautiful. . . ." The
creature took the cake, lifted it to her mouth, and
smiling put it down on the grass. At that moment,
Euphrosine Gellanbé thrust out her two fists and
cried in a voice full of innocence, gentleness, and
nostalgia, which contrasted strangely with the
two war clubs she was brandishing: "Black friends,
my sweet, sneering, play-acting blacks, do you
know what? . . . Sometimes I wonder why God
created the white man, and it plagues me, here in
my big head. . . ."

Everyone laughed at the question that was
plaguing her and at her way of speaking. And

one of the men answered briskly, for the saltwater
folk hold that a man's tongue is made to be used:
"Dear woman, don't blame God for creating the
tiger . . . thank him for not giving him
wings. . . ."

Since the yellow woman's arrival, Sanga, the
Mandingo chief, had sat back, dominating the
scene with his heavy, somber, unmoving eyes,
which seemed to look upon the affairs of this
world from an infinite distance. He was blue-black,
with hard, dry limbs and a stern bearing, rigid
with the sense of his importance. The incisions on
his face gave him the look of a malignant idol. His
lips moved as in a dream, and everyone expected
him to say something appropriate to the sadness
of the hour, to utter one of those phrases that
make you glad again to be a black in the land of
men. But turning toward the stranger, he said
simply: "Woman, what is your name?"

The creature hesitated. She bowed her head
and raised her emaciated arms in bewilderment.
She didn't know, she said, because no one had
called her by name for many years. But people
used to call her Solitude. Taking her pipe out of
her mouth, an old woman observed that that wasn't

a human name, no, certainly not. And as though to prove that she belonged to the human race, the creature hastened to reply: "Rosalie, yes, they called me Rosalie, and some called me Two-Souls . . ." And in a sententious tone she concluded: ". . . because of my eyes, you see." Then for the first time the Mandingo's face came to life. His eyes shone with a veiled, cruel light, and looking about him with the weighty disenchantment of one who bore the destinies of men on his shoulders, he said bitterly: "Who can speak of a name? Which of you here can claim to have a name? . . . If you've lost your African name, you might just as well be called No-Name; what do you say, Cousin Médor? What do you say, Dog-Tick and Big-Snout?"

And going back to the woman who had been fished out of the river:

"Tell me. Are you completely mad?"

She thought it over and answered: "No, not completely."

"Are you sick?"

"I used to be ridden by the spirits of animals; but they've left me now."

"And what color are you?"

Tears flowed down the creature's smiling cheeks,

her jaw drooped, and her eyes took on a tinge of
sadness. Raising her hands to her face, she looked
at her wet fingers, glistening with tears. The smile
descended from her eyes to her lips, which parted,
disclosing her small childlike teeth. Someone muttered with embarrassment: "I like the way she
smiles." Others wagged their heads, uttering a
soft delighted keppe at the bottom of their throats.
Sensing the sweetness and fragility of this cool,
damp night, the Mandingo nodded gravely and
said: "Look . . . the diamond that was in her
heart is glittering on her face." After these words
the night took on a sumptuous silky blue, which
blended with the creature's silence. The sounds of
the forest died down, and each of the runaways
felt that he too was part of this silence, which was
more immense than heaven and earth together. A
few scratched their temples, others shook their
lowered heads, like oxen fretting dreamily under
the yoke. One woman who had understood nothing
turned to the creature and said in a voice trembling with fear: "You're not angry with us, I
hope?"

The Mandingo heaved a deep sigh, and those
who knew his pathways, who discerned on his face
the trails of his beautiful black thoughts, knew

that he was going to utter a "final" word, one of those saltwater sayings that make you glad again to be a black in the land of men: "Listen," he said with an imperceptible smile. "Listen, little yellow leaf . . . we are no more than a calabash full of water, not enough to put out the fire. But does that mean water is useless against fire? . . . Would anyone say that, would anyone? . . ."

Far down on the slopes, not far from the sea-shore, an animal howled, and, echo re-echoing echo, its cry rose up to the mountain, which sucked it into its folds, transforming it into damp night and silence. A stifled laugh was heard in the darkness. A young Congo woman was talking to herself, while thrusting a stick of incense into the coals. Those around her were sleeping, all was silence in her heart and the silence frightened her. Her only company was a stout matron with hair like a gray sponge, who was sitting regally by the fireside, a sleeping child on her broad back. From time to time the matron turned her head to contemplate a shape that was stretched out under a blanket nearby; then once more she became a mountain of darkness, traversed by the unsteady glow of the dying fire. Between the two women

lay an old she-dog with one paw over her muzzle.
She was infinitely battered and worn, but a number of puppies clung to her flanks like fruit, like
green leaves clinging to a dead tree. All her life
she had wandered about the mountains, she was
unacquainted with the black man's smell. That
was why they had taken her in and helped her to
bear her litter. The young woman had been born
under other skies; she was dreaming of Africa,
revolving a few images that had stayed with her,
the precious fragments of an old world. Suddenly
she returned to the present and was startled at
the sight of the sleeping camp, the dying fire, the
litter of puppies at her feet, the taciturn matron,
the yellow creature under the blanket, and the
impenetrable wall that surrounded the camp with
its thousands of unknown trees, plants, and insects, in the midst of which she would have to live
and die without ever being able to give them a
name. Buffeted by a remote eddy of salt water,
the young woman stood up, took a few tottering
steps, approached the shape under the blanket,
and said: "She's crying, she's crying in her sleep.
Oh, look, it's so strange. . . ."

At this the aged matron with the child bounded
over to the Congo girl and whispered in a tone of

command: "Peace!" And without further explanation she drove the girl away, waving her arms as
though shooing chickens. The matron's name was
Euphrosine Gellanbé, an inversion of her first
master's name. Next morning Euphrosine told
her companions that she had gone for forty-two
years without shedding a tear—from the day she
had landed on the island to the day when she had
taken to the woods. And that was why she had
said: "Peace."

7

EVERY DAY Solitude felt emptier and lighter, like
a bubble shot through with shimmering lights.
Long long ago she had learned to distrust the
words that came out of her mouth: they were mirrors that fell at her feet, shattering her reflection.
She moved soundlessly among the runaway blacks,
like a soap bubble revolving in the mansions of the
sky, silently mirroring everything about her. She
never opened her mouth or moved her tongue of
darkness, except in direct response to the living.
When she returned to the camp after gathering
herbs on the mountain, she would whistle from far
off. Raising her head like a baying wolf, looking
up fearfully at the tops of the tall trees, she would
cry: "It's me. Don't shoot, it's me." And invariably a voice that seemed to fall straight from the

sky, from the blue-veined foliage, would reply:
"Who me, in God's name?" And Solitude would
bow her head and answer: "It's me, the woman
who fell into the river. . . ."

Every day she went to the woods and came back
with medicinal herbs, wild fruit, roots, leaves that
had the properties of tobacco, and clusters of red
and yellow dingdé berries, which when steeped
in boiling, slightly salted water, yielded an excellent oil. Impressed by her knowledge of plants, the
women asked the name of each one and were
amazed to hear of the uses to which they could
be put. When she had finished answering questions, she closed her mouth with an air of finality
and wandered about the camp, carefully register-
ing each face, the exact intonation of each voice,
and above all the bearing of these living bodies.
Certain Congo gestures sank into her so deeply
that they became hers, she imitated them with an
innate grace, an ease which may have been the
consequence of old habit, of the thousands of times
she had looked at a particular person in a particular hut on the du Parc plantation, long long
ago. But despite her efforts, the African dances
remained alien to her. Wrapping a pagne tightly
around her loins, she would try to move like the

Congo women; in vain; invariably she would surprise an amused smile on their faces. No sooner
had she captured a gesture, an inclination of the
head, a way of holding out her open hand as
though to receive a jar, a light burden, or the
tender caress of the air, than a false movement of
her bust would reduce the splendor to nothing.
And another difficulty was that no two of these
women were alike; each had her own gait, her own
dance steps, her own special way of pronouncing
the saltwater phrases. Some were small and black,
others had freckles all over their faces, still others
were long and smooth and red, like trees whose
bark had been stripped. They laughed, they made
fun of one another; each seemed to find ground
for superiority in her origins, whether Ibo or
Mane or Beni, Fanti, or Nganguélé, whether she
had come from the kingdom of Mossi or of Bornu,
from a land of plains, savannas or lakes, or from
one of those numerous green islands somehow contained within the big Congo Island, just as the
eyes of a child are contained within the glance of
an adult. They made up proverbs and verses at
the expense of those who had not been born in their
village, who had not bathed in the true river. In
the presence of a ponderous old woman with a red

bead in one nostril, they would say: "Dahomey woman: so much guile, she'll cheat herself and calmly smile." The old woman would roll her eyes with indignation while others chortled with glee. And Solitude would feel emptier and lighter than ever, blown by the furious wind of time. All her old sorrows came back to her, and in an instant flash she would ask herself where Africa could be: "Tell me, where is it, where?"

The name of the woman with the bead was Euphrosine. She was a mountain of a woman, always sweating and joyful, quivering and alert, with cheeks like hills and beautiful arms that flowed like rivers. At first Solitude was unable to look at her without laughing and crying and forming all sorts of words behind her sealed lips. On her back Euphrosine carried a little ball, a marvelous creature all of black milk, who seemed to be always asleep, cradled by the enormous woman's gently rolling gait. Gravely she nursed the infant, whom she had taken from a dead woman, squeezing her breasts, which were as broad and flat as tobacco leaves, as though milking a cow. Despite her gray hair, she still gave a thin frothy milk, thanks to a medicine chosen by Sanga: a few

brown pellets which she took every morning with
her eyes closed, anxiously begging the gods for a
last remnant of youth. Everything about her was
marvelously Congo, not the least being the obscuri-
ties of her speech and certain private eccentricities. For instance, she had no intention of returning home on a ship in the usual manner of
saltwater blacks. No, she would go on foot, underground, through the maze of tunnels used by the
Dahomey spirits, which all lead back to the village.
Her profession of faith was greeted with gales of
laughter. The others ridiculed her heresy, pre-
dicting that she would get lost in the underground
labyrinth. But Euphrosine only shrugged her
great shoulders and shook herself like a lazy, con-
tented mare. Then, smiling faintly, her nostrils
dilated with tenderness, she would sing a song addressed to everyone and no one, or perhaps to the
destiny that is written in the heavens:

Who says I will never see the River Niger again?
    Is it the Tree?
    Is it the Madman?
Is it the Tortoise or my Mother?

When she heard such things, Solitude's mouth
opened and discordant sounds came out; tears ran

down her cheeks and her companions moved away in fear, asking each other anxiously: "Is she of this world?" Some of the women shook their heads and muttered knowingly: "You greet the living and the dead answer you." And turning her trembling candid eyes, somewhat discolored by age, in Solitude's direction, Euphrosine seemed to discover her presence as though seeing her for the first time that day. "Good morning," she would say with a smile. "What are you doing with the spirits of the night?" But the general anxiety was audible in her voice, and Solitude was sick at heart. The staring eyes around her laid her bare and plunged her back into the old waters. She lost her footing, an eddy carried her off, she was gone. When night fell, the old dreams came back to her. She was a yellow dog in the streets of Pointe-à-Pitre, naked, running on all fours, her tongue hanging down to the ground. And when she awoke, she hovered in doubt: was she Solitude who had dreamt she was a yellow dog, or was she a dog dreaming it was a human woman named Solitude? She arose, watched the black woman's admirable movements and imitated them in a frenzy of joy or sorrow. But her doubt about herself was never quite dispelled. . . .

One day as she was thus hovering between
dream and waking, the camp was alerted by the
wailing of the conch horns. Cries, shots, and the
faint barking of dogs could be heard through the
woods. While the aged, the children, and most of
the women made for the heights, Solitude and
several other women followed the men down toward the Goyave. Three were in the lead, one
armed with a club, one with a bayonet affixed to
a stick, one with a machete. They brandished their
weapons in the air and howled. Now and then Solitude looked around. A black face motioned to her
to go back. But she shook her head and went on
down the slope, determined to stay with Euphrosine Gellanbé, who waddled heavily onward amid
the jagged rocks, the infant clinging to the enormous back as a lizard clings to a wall. When they
reached the river, the skirmish was over. The only
enemy to be seen was a young white man on the
opposite bank, firing calmly across the river. Half-
hidden by a tree trunk, he was wearing the green
uniform of the chasseurs, with a wig and leggings
and a plumed hat. At every shot he burst out
laughing. The blacks dragged their wounded into
a copse to escape his fire. As she looked on the
scene, Solitude felt herself hovering between dog

and woman. Even in the tips of her long trembling fingers she had the same sickening feeling. With mingled joy and sadness she took a last look at the world around her: the soft half-light of the forest, the blue spots that fell from the sky and whirled through her head, Euphrosine squatting behind a bush, puffing and sweating, with that little black ball nestling below the gray sponge of her hair. A blood-stained machete was lying in the grass. She stooped, picked it up with her fingertips, and ran down to the river, shouting: "Kill me, kill me, I say . . . oh, kill me." With an incredulous smile the fighting men watched the creature in the weird, semi-saltwater costume negligently moving her machete through the air like a parasol. Holding in one hand the flowered curtain she took for a pagne, she leapt from stone to stone, stammering words of supplication. Her machete rose and fell, sometimes coming dangerously close to her cheeks. Still behind his tree, the white soldier watched her with the same stunned look as the motionless blacks on the opposite ba¬k. "Kill me, kill me," she repeated, staring at him out of her enormous eyes. She fell into the water, grabbed hold of a flat stone, and staggered up the grassy slope. The soldier made a move as though

131

to raise his gun; but she was already on him. For the last time she cried sorrowfully: "Oh kill me, I say, kill me," and plunged her machete into his belly.

An hour later it seemed to her that she was still on the bank of the Goyave, contemplating the fragile architecture of the world for the last time. Men had crossed the river and taken the machete, which she was holding as though in a dream. They had brought her back to the Little Guinea shore, and with an arm around her waist someone had led her up the path. Branches brushed gently across her face. Suddenly she saw Euphrosine Gellanbé beside her, drawing her slowly upward, her neck straining and sweating, laboring up the slope like a weary but determined horse. And then Solitude had wished strength into her legs. When they reached camp, Solitude took a few steps on her own and sat down calmly by the fire, suddenly attentive to what was going on around her: the pity in these doomed faces, the lament of the human voices, the joyous crackling of the leaves and branches, which seemed glad that in an instant, the time it takes to draw a breath, they would cease to be. She looked without seeing, neither weeping nor smiling, furtively clutching at her fist now and then, as though to make sure she was there. All around her witnesses were telling the story, leaping from imaginary stone to stone. An old woman who had just returned from the mountain came up to her and said timidly, as though asking a question: "Kill me, kill me?" Then suddenly confused, she burst into tears and went away.

Euphrosine took Solitude by the elbow as though leading a blind woman, and, turning her cold eyes toward the flames, hissed softly between her teeth: "Well, how does your living body feel?" When the creature did not reply, but merely looked at her out of great tearful eyes, Euphrosine took her by the shoulder and said to her in a guttural, muffled voice, as though determined at all costs to convince her of heaven knew what: "Here you are back again, back again with us, black woman, black woman, black woman. . . ."

The days that followed were luminous. The dry season was at an end. Yellow shapes rolled through the sky, rising and falling in multicolored droplets that caressed the back of your eyes. Far below, the sea smiled in its sleep, the mountain crags were silver, the trees glittered and breathed indistinct sounds, and the living skins of the black women seemed covered with mirrors. Everything was so new on the earth, so fresh to your eyes, your fingers, your nostrils that it was hard to believe; you couldn't help wondering if it was all a dream. When Solitude walked slowly through the grass, the soles of her feet tingled with astonishment. And when she ate cassava cake, a spoonful of Congo soup, or merely a square of malanga soaked in oil, her mouth received it like a rare unknown dish that really had no place here in the land of men. . . . Sometimes a look of life came into her eyes, and the Dahomey woman said to her on a note of feigned jealousy: "Watch out. You're getting to be like a quail in the spring." Like everything around her, these words went to her heart and shivering in her bones Solitude protested gravely: "Oh, I still stink worse than a caterpillar." And running a finger over the pink welts on Solitude's ankle, Euphrosine murmured in a voice full of tenderness. "No, my love. You only stink a little, just a little. . . ."

At daybreak on April 7 a courier from below reported that several corvettes had anchored in the bay and that uniforms belonging to every branch of service were to be seen in Petit-Bourg.

An old man in a dashiki began to stagger like a bull struck with a mallet. His face was marked with death. Women wept together, burying their long pink and black fingers in each other's hair. One by one the night shadows faded and yellow threads fell from the sky. Solitude smiled inwardly. Her smile was like a light breeze on the sea, pushing a ripple before it, scarcely more than a wrinkle on the still waters of her soul. But the breeze met an adverse wind, the sea threw up cold bitter waves, and to her astonishment Solitude discovered the Mandingo. A green ceremonial band on his broad, creased forehead, he was sitting bolt upright by the fire, his legs crossed in the grass. Several others were with him. Euphrosine was watching him as in a dream. Her slow movements had the solemn restraint of a last parting. Gravely Solitude contemplated the Dahomey woman. Her friend's mouth seemed to be full of water, her nostrils breathed despair and angrily blew it out. "Can they?" she said. "Will they?" All eyes turned toward her and she was seized with embarrassment. Bowing her head between her mountainous shoulders, she expressed her naive astonishment at those black men in uniform who were going to attack their poor black brothers.

There were smiles, and the Mandingo answered
with cold sarcasm scarcely tempered by deference:
"Dear woman, maybe those big black beasts have
chafed at the bit so long they've begun to like it.
Maybe . . ." And the man grinned, shrugged his
shoulders, and shook his head with infinite sadness, as though the barb of his own words had
pierced his heart. Rediscovering the weight of
their chains and the power that certain white men
had in their eyes, several of the runaways bowed
their heads with a sigh, reflecting that the black
race was lost for all eternity . . . *a fallen race,
yes, I say, a fallen race.* . . .

The Mandingo's throat swelled with sadness
and a soft, guttural sound came out of his open
mouth, as though he were babbling in his sleep.
Maybe he was going to say something, a saltwater
phrase, just the phrase that was needed that day,
in this hour and this moment, the phrase which
for the last time would make them glad, and give
them the strength, to be black in the land of men.
But his jaw sagged, his eyes covered with a gray
mist, and words without radiance fell from the
worn leather of his lips. All this, he said, in a nasal
monotone that seemed to come from far away—all
this was happening because of the mystery of

white thought; all those who entered into it were lost indeed; they became shadows, puppets in the white man's dream. They ceased to be, it was as if they had never been.

The others exchanged looks of consternation, shaken by this vision of the white man's magic. And those who remembered their chains, and the power that certain white men had in their eyes, felt the ground opening beneath their feet. . . .

Solitude's face turned ashen. Slowly her hands rose to her throat, her cheeks, her absent, puppet eyes. Hearing her faint cry, the Mandingo leaned over her and said with a smile that his words had not been for her, for she had always had a beautiful heart, a black woman's heart, in her breast. Very gravely and thoughtfully, several others nodded in agreement. And one, to set the seal on what had been said, sang out with a triumphant laugh: "Kill me, hee-hee."

8

TWO DAYS LATER, after the destruction of the
camp, a silent band made their way to the heights,
hoisting themselves from branch to branch, crossing chasms and gorges, skirting the forest on narrow trails, over a carpet of ferns that masked the
crevasses. Gone were the huts and garden patches,
and the heroes lay by the banks of the Goyave,
shorn of their heads, which, spitted on pikes, were
being paraded around the island. The Mandingo
had left instructions that the survivors should
make a war drum out of his skin, lest his doctrine
die with him, but even that had not been possible.
Luckily Solitude, in her days as a dog, had discovered countless fox holes and caves inhabited
only by bats. Without meaning to, without even
knowing what she was doing—or so it is said—she

led the forlorn band, which dwindled with each passing day. First the old people died; then the few children, the "small fry" as the masters used to call them; then the fatter women, carried off by the dampness of the forest. All were buried deep in the ground, their heads pointing toward Africa, ready to take flight. Only three humble Congos, who had always obeyed, and two black women, Toupie and Médélices, were left. From morning to night they looked to Solitude, who closed her eyes, rested her hands on her breast in order to hear her beautiful black heart, and grunted softly deep down in her throat, in the comforting manner of Sanga the Mandingo.

Toward the end of April 1799, the group settled on the heights of La Soufrière, among the devilbirds, at the dividing line beyond which all mineral and vegetable life ceased. Above them lay the terraces of the volcano, its hot springs and its rumblings. Their bodies were spotted yellow from the clouds of sulphur which the wind blew down over the slopes. At their feet lay a Guadeloupe they did not know, with its hills flattened by the distance, its valleys clogged with mist, its cane fields along the shore and its offshore islands that looked like specks of foam. The large islands in

---

the distance, Martinique, Désirade, and Montserrat, each with its volcano, danced in the hot air. Sometimes a ring of clouds surrounded the fugitives, then, descending on the world like a curtain, lifted them up into the sky. When hunger overtook them, they would scramble down the old lava trails to look for food at the edge of the forest. When night fell, they would prowl around the plantations, grabbing what came their way, a hen, a pig, a goat, severing its head at one stroke, before it could even think of crying out. Now and then they would raid a storehouse, taking whole bunches of bananas, sacks of malanga, sweet potatoes, arm-long yams, and bundles of purple-streaked sugar cane, the juiciest kind and a comfort in their misery. Once, not far from Grand Val, they found themselves surrounded by torches. Overcome by exhaustion and a cloying sadness, Solitude ran toward the lights, whirling her machete in the night. Another day in the woods they came face to face with a detachment of soldiers searching for lazy citizens. The little band became legendary, feared throughout the countryside. Traps were set for them, they were chased for hours on end. Followed by three humble Congos who had always obeyed and by two black women, Toupie and Médélices, Solitude flung herself at the dogs and armed men. When it was all over, she looked with surprise at her dripping machete, her blood-stained hands, and the stunned eyes of her companions. Then she wept softly, understanding nothing. And when alarmed at her tears the others caressed her, she frowned through her tears, and grunted softly, deep down in her throat. . . .

Weary of living in the sulphurous caverns of the volcano, the fugitives looked for new quarters. Following the Black River past Nez Cassé, La Matéliane, and Le Petit-sans-Toucher, they made their way to the "forbidden" forest, which was said to be haunted by spirits of the dead. There they hunted the wild pig, trapped agoutis and mountain doves, and sounded the hollow stick at the least sign of life: two shorts for game, one long for anything human. The moss, the tangled lianas, the trees with their flying buttresses were eternally coated with gray dust—a fit dwelling place for ghosts. Far overhead a curtain of blue, green, and scarlet leaves, which might have been cut from colored glass, distilled a mottled, unreal light. But for the present the dead souls, intimidated by the new arrivals, kept their distance. Their presence could only be surmised by certain signs—lights, balls of fire, sighs that rose from the ground at night, mingled with the chirping of the crickets, the moaning of the trees as they stretched in their sleep, the dry explosions as the sandbox trees burst their pods and flung their seeds into the darkness. One night the dead cried out for hours, all together, with the plaintive voices of the children, friends, brothers, and sisters fallen by the banks of the Goyave. And the living were at a loss, wondering how to answer, how to be silent, how to endure the voices of these headless blacks, who had been unable to find the road to Africa. Weeks passed. Occasionally a flute sounded in the moonlight, at the hour when the trade winds fall back into the sea. The ghostly musician began with a trill, then a softly breathed melody spun itself like a long silk thread into the indifference of the night. The spirits of the dead danced around the fire like mosquitoes, and the fugitives huddled together in fear. Now and then, recognizing the departed shapes, one of them would stand up and sit down, stand up and sit down, speechless with terror. Suddenly Solitude decided in favor of the living. Crossing middle finger and forefinger, she raised her right hand and, defeated by her frail exorcism, the dead souls dispersed. She had seen that gesture long long ago, perhaps in a dream, she couldn't remember. . . .

One day when they were pursuing a wild sow, they encountered a spirit of the dead, or so they thought. Bristling with arrows, the beast, followed by her young, vanished into a clump of lianas, ferns, and strangely shaped arborescences resembling globes, bluish domes, or parasols with stays, at once branches and roots, hanging down to the ground. With the slow solemnity of giants, great tree trunks emerged from the green moss. A trail led through the tangle into a clearing. Two or three hens were strolling about, cackling, in the shade of a grass hut decorated with drawings of animals. Here and there painted calabashes and earthenware dishes were strewn about. A turtle-leg stool stood beside a blackened stone fireplace, and a bone flute lay on the ground nearby. The air seemed liquid, and as though from the bottom of a well one could see a small circle of sky between the treetops. The thicket parted and a dead Congo in a pagne emerged. A little man. He had yellow bracelets on both wrists and his hair was sprinkled with bright-colored seeds. He raised his ghostly

arms, showing the pink palms of his hands, and
murmured in a tone of intense fear: "Brothers,
brothers, I give you the friendship of my hands."
He seemed to have stepped out of an ethereal, en-
chanted comedy, and Solitude was afraid he
would vanish in a multicolored cloud. Toupie,
Médélices, and the three Congos went up to him
and smothered him with their caresses, laughing
and crying at once. There had been no need of
words: The stranger's eyes, toes, and fingers had
told them the truth of his being. Solitude remained off to one side, pleasantly bewildered, as
though her body were floating amid the trees.
When they led the frightened little man with the
big startled eyes to her, she felt wretchedly yellow
and burst into a strident laugh. All that day,
when Solitude looked at the sky, at the trees or
her old companions, it seemed to her that her heart
was the heart of a black woman and that her eyes
saw all things as Sanga had seen them. But when
she looked at the flute player, she wanted to weep
bitter tears for herself and for this "wandering
soul" in his desert island with his moist, frightened
smile, his elongated eyes on a level with his forehead, and his beautiful saltwater arms that it
would be so good, so right, so necessary to touch.

And then she felt that she had grown yellow again, yellow and frail and naked, as she had been long ago before she began to live. Her eyelids fluttered and she moved hesitantly, colliding with trees, scraping against leaves and branches. Her companions were alarmed, but with the coming of night she calmed down. She sat beside the fire, and she no longer feared looking at the man: Her heart would not stop beating. Negligently she turned toward him, her eyes met those of the "wandering soul," and so they both remained, spellbound, their arms limp and an incredulous smile on their lips.

A little later, in the middle of the night, she woke up with the same indefinable feeling of uneasiness, the same astonishment in her throat. She saw the little man at a distance of eight or ten paces from her, watching her and scratching the top of his head thoughtfully. At that moment compassion descended upon the earth, a strange dark compassion that spoke of all things without giving them a name. Solitude stood up and, smiling, took a few steps toward the man. With racing heart she went halfway, then, when her legs would no longer support her, sat down in the grass. The man was still scratching his head in silence, daring neither to look at her nor to avert his eyes. And that was how their first night of love passed. So Solitude learned the mystery of Man Bobette and what had happened between the child she had been and Man Bobette; and from that moment on it seemed to her that everything was in order, regardless of whether Man Bobette was rotting under some stump or journeying on the ship that was to carry her back to Africa. From time to time she dozed off, awoke with a cry, and opened her eyes on a world steeped in darkness: the trees, the beasts, her companions, and the little black man, the wandering soul, who was still scratching his head, wondering what new thing was happening to him in this country. . . .

Maimouni remained a riddle to her, a source of endless questions. Watching him move around the clearing, she had the impression that his whole life reduced itself to this quiet patch of ground, barely large enough for a hut, a bit of a garden, a goat and a few chickens, in the image of the patch of African soil that he carried in his heart and that hid the rest of the world from him. His eyes did not see the dead and took little interest in the living. His only tie with Guadeloupe was Solitude herself, a frail adventitious root. From her he learned a few words of Creole, drawn from the bottommost depths of servitude, and these words were his first link with this island and its strange customs. But when he pronounced them, the words had a strange ring in Solitude's ears. Shifting from his silence to his words, the mystery of Maimouni divided and subdivided into minute shadowy droplets, raising new questions in her heart. In telling her of his village, Maimouni spoke of an enormous mountain, a hundred times higher, he said, than La Soufrière, and crowned not with flames but with an eternal white substance that glittered in the sun. He also told her that he had been a slave in Africa, enslaved since the beginning of the world to the tribe that had sold him to the white men. That had happened at the beginning, he said, just after the word had been given to the crowned crane. Yes, that was how it had happened. For a long time Solitude was unable to believe him, for his words were directly contrary to the Mandingo's doctrine. But the man provided exact details. Every morning, for instance, the masters beat the recalcitrants on the backs of their necks with a small club—light, restrained blows—to put their spirit of revolt to

sleep. Maimouni spoke of the little club with a
smile, as though it were perfectly natural in this
world to bow your head before your blood brothers, throughout innumerable births and rebirths,
and finally to be traded for a barrel of rum. But
try as she might, Solitude could see nothing amus-
ing in the flute player's story. It made her very
sad; how could there be room for this little club
in the marvelous life of Congo Island? Questions
fell on her face like the cold, dark, salty raindrops
that fall in the middle of the night. Sometimes,
for a brief moment, she saw herself as a fly, caught
in the Mandingo's dream. And then she asked herself: Was this not a white thought? Was she not,
on the contrary, part of the white man's dream,
just like those poor niggers in uniform in whose
heads the white man had laid their eggs? Then
everything became confused behind her forehead,
the words of the Mandingo, the comings and
goings of a little club as heavy and as light as the
world, and the solitary song of a flute rising up in
the night. She opened her eyes wide, clenched her
fists, and told herself with a smile that she really
didn't amount to much in the land of men if she
didn't even know in whose dream she was.

Maimouni had lost all sense of time; he had no

idea how many days, months, or years he had
passed on this island, in this clearing at the bottom of a well, which was itself an island. Trees had
been born and grown in the interval, the sky had
changed its shape and color and his hair had
turned white. Here, he sometimes said, the earth
was better than in Mozambique; it was singularly
firm and fertile, though perhaps a bit too rich for
his taste. And he would bend down over one of his
secret gardens, a long red trench veiled by creepers and ferns, in which he had planted all manner
of vegetables and roots pellmell in the African
manner, in order that each plant might sing its
song correctly under the sky. He shook his head
knowingly, and his narrowed eyes took on a distant, dreamlike look: yes, he repeated, though a
bit too rich for his taste. And the fugitives marveled at his manners, the delicacy with which he
handled his hoe, his firestones, his pot, in which
he was always cooking good things, seasoned with
incense ash, his own invention. They loved the
gray temples on his child's face, and his round,
wandering, fragile, astonished tadpole's eyes,
which looked fearfully on all things, as though
this man had just landed, as though he had been
sold and delivered the day before. . . . In the

evening, when he had finished tilling his land, shut
the animals up in their pens, and prepared one of
those fine saltwater dishes that go straight to your
soul, the runaways touched his elbow and said:
"Brother, speak a few shining words, throw a
little light on our shoulders." The man would
tremble, turn his face in all directions, and say
a few words in Creole, smiling in spite of himself
at the immensity of his ignorance: "Forgive me,"
he would say. "Ladies and gentlemen, forgive me;
words are far above me, and the things that happen are too big for Maimouni's mouth." Regret-
fully the fugitives would answer: "Brother, the
heavens know that the word can be no bigger than
the man, for it is all contained in his mouth." And
Maimouni would shake his narrow forehead, and
murmur with an oracular assurance that filled
them with astonishment: "Eia, I know nothing,
but I do know there are woods behind the woods,
and I know that all speech began with the crowned
crane; for it was the crowned crane who first said:
I speak." The runaways would smile indulgently,
for it seemed to them that the little man was looking on the world for the first time, like an infant
incapable of distinguishing the gentle from the
terrible or the majestic. But Solitude was not of

150

that opinion; she even had a feeling that Maimouni's eyes had seen all things here below, known
all joys and sorrows and grandeurs. This feeling,
as light and elusive as gossamer, had come to her
one day when danger had threatened. Shots had
been heard from not too far off. The fugitives had
taken shelter behind a rock, whence they peered
out over the surrounding slopes, but Maimouni
had stayed calmly in his garden, preoccupied with
his plants, as though the shots belonged to another
world that did not concern him, or as though he
had resolved that death should surprise him in the
midst of his yams, Carib cabbages, and malangas.
When the alarm had passed, he had looked up over
his hoe. Seeing the yellow woman in a sweat, he
had gone over to her and pulled a lock of hair on
the nape of her neck, as he sometimes did. With a
sigh of impatience Solitude had asked him: "Why
are you pulling my hair?" Maimouni's eyes had
sparkled with heavenly light and he had replied
in his slightly pompous Creole—each day he was
learning a little more, with the same application
as he put into his yams, Carib cabbages, and malangas—"Why shouldn't I pull your hair? Aren't
you a girl?"

* * *

Solitude knew she was with child. One night she dreamed that first her head, then her shoulders, her arms, and the rest of her sank into Maimouni's body, until the whole of her was covered with a beautiful black skin. She was happy, drunk on the warm blood in which she was bathed from head to foot. For a few days she said nothing of her metamorphosis, of the tender bones, the skin, and hair that were growing inside her. But the little man knew, he watched her out of the still water of his great luminous eyes and touched her belly with the sureness, the delicacy, the mysterious elegance with which he treated his garden. Under his touch, beams of colored light and luminous expanses of water came into being, and branches burst into bud. Solitude seemed to see the petals of a glance beginning to open. Seeing her surprise, he said: "The father's hand is a sun to the child." At night, before giving her his seed, he bade her think of her child, compose an image of this or that precious organ or limb, so as to complete the formative action of the spirits. He attached special importance to the nails, the fingers, the harmonious mold of the torso, the ears, teeth, and lips, and, perhaps most of all, to the roundness and firmness of the liver. But he was never able to say what sort of heart he wanted for the child. He could not wish it an African heart, which would be useless in a foreign country, and still less could he resign himself to a white, black, or mulatto heart beating to the obscure rhythm of Guadeloupe. At first Solitude had smiled at these fantasies. But a strange thing happened: The man grew sad and his Creole words left him; he had difficulty in saying them, and unknown songs rose to his lips as he lay with her at night. Then he spoke of his own flesh, apologizing at length for his native idiom, with sighs of regret that suddenly made the unfinished child tremble. . . .

9

————————

Early one afternoon, on a day like other days, a peal of thunder shook the great trees, sending a rain of leaves down on the astonished fugitives. The animals whimpered and slunk away into the copse. Surprised in her sleep, a dead woman suddenly flew up to the sky, her breasts flapping like wings. As the noise grew louder, one of the Congos climbed a mahogany tree and reported smoke on the heights and spirals of black smoke, like rings blown from a cigar. It must be a war, he said. But what war?

This cannonade on the Côte-sous-le-Vent was the beginning of the end of an episode in history which, though unknown to the fugitives, was to be their death. It had begun beyond the seas many years before, on 6 Pluviôse of the year II, the day when slavery in the French colonies was abolished. The Convention had resigned itself to this measure in the secret hope that the news of it would spread to the plantations of the British West Indies from the Virgin Islands to Jamaica, and provoke a revolution. When the vote had gone his way, Danton, beside himself with joy, unmasked his batteries: "Gentlemen," he said, "England is dead." Seven years later, the peace treaty with England opened the seas to sugar and put an end to the brief freedom of the blacks. The day after it was signed, a large fleet put out from Brest: two ships of the line, four frigates, a supply ship, and three transports carrying veterans of the campaigns of Italy, Austria, and Prussia, all able soldiers commanded by some of Bonaparte's finest officers. General Richepance first put into Pointe-à-Pitre, whose black National Guards, in response to an impeccably republican speech, let themselves be disarmed without a murmur. They were quickly stripped of their uniforms and thrown naked into the holds of the transports, packed like herrings in a keg.

This happened on May 6 of the year of grace 1802. Early in the afternoon a few days later the squadron appeared off Basse-Terre and was

greeted by the thunder of all the black batteries
on the coast. . . .

Up in his mahogany tree, the Congo reported
troops of blacks moving about the country, shots
in the distance, and plantations burning like bales
of straw. Somewhere in the darkness of the forest,
a leaf sparkled and a jar broke at the edge of a
spring. Solitude wound a wide band of cloth
around her belly, crossed the ends and tied them
in front, just above her child, tightening the knot
with all her strength. Maimouni, who did not
understand, made no move to stop her from going.
Drunk with weariness, the companions supported
the little yellow woman, parted the branches and
brambles before her, and picked her up gently
when the weight of her belly made her fall. Night
came quickly, turning the whole world blue. The
cannonade stopped. A little later, on a road
shrouded in darkness, they saw hundreds of soldiers and field niggers brandishing torches, guns,
and long ox goads. The French had landed at Le
Baillif and were getting reinforcements from
Pointe-à-Pitre. These men had come to cut them
off and, God willing, stop them for a few hours at

the crossing of the Grand'Anse River. When she reached the rebel camp, Solitude collapsed into a puddle the size and shape of her body; it was her own sweat. Unknown men bent over her, murmuring her name, but she could not answer. Behind the field niggers, unfamiliar figures were gathered around the campfire. An old sergeant of the Guard was crying, beating his forehead, and accusing himself of having misled the men of his race, put them on the path to slavery and death. She saw a mulatto citizen with a Phrygian cap and double cockade, and even a yellow lady of fashion, still dripping with earrings and bracelets and wearing a little beribboned corset. All were wild-eyed and gray with fatigue, soldiers and field niggers, mulatto citizens, and humble, silent Congos; all had the same look of terror and bewilderment, of vague, impersonal suffering, as though they no longer belonged to themselves and already saw themselves in the big invisible hands of the white men. She dozed off, and as she was sleeping Maimouni's fingers touched her forehead and closed eyelids. When she returned to the world an hour later, the wandering soul was stretched out beside her, caressing the child with a slow, gentle, regular movement, as calmly as if he had been

157

dreaming in his woods, two steps from his yams, his Carib cabbages, and his malangas. She raised herself on one elbow, and turned to him with frightened, sorrowful eyes, full of boundless pity. But Maimouni shook his head gracefully and murmured with his usual smile: "The good things don't happen every day, you know."

She heard a military band, fifes, drums, and cymbals, playing the traditional tune: "*Where can you be better off than in the bosom of your family?*" Then the enemy column appeared in the gray of dawn, halfway up the hill, preceded by a black cymbal player in a Turkish uniform bedizened with gold braid. At the first volley, the hill was covered with batteries, firing grapeshot, bounding cannon balls, and long chains that flew as though on wings, spreading water and blood behind the sandbags that had been piled up in haste during the night. Not far from Solitude an old woman swung a machete over her bald head and cried out in a hoarse voice: "*Vive la mort. Jésus, vive la mort.*" Maimouni's eyes rested on Solitude, on the unfinished child. He had not so much as a glance for the joys and sorrows and grandeurs of the battle. Solitude was astonished. Then the wandering soul slumped, and she felt his gentle weight on her shoulders, still so near and already so infinitely far . . .

Solitude started down the hill, clinging to rocks, bushes, clumps of flowers. From time to time she shook her yellow fist in feeble derision and let out angry inarticulate cries that ended in sobs. Falling to the ground, she rolled down the slope and lay still, with arms outspread. She saw shadows against the light, men and women scrambling down the hill, wildly gesticulating, and she saw the faraway ecstasy on their sweaty faces. She picked up a bayonet and began to run, her belly wobbling in all directions. They pursued the French to Trou-aux-Chiens, to Fond-Bananier, to Capesterre. News reached them: victory communiqués. The whites were falling back at Belost, Ducharmoy, and Fort Saint-Charles; they were even threatened with yellow fever, which had burst out of their perverse blood. Drunk with a new hope so old they did not recognize it, some of the runaway blacks kissed the ground, weeping and crying out: "My country, my country, my country . . ."

On May 19, 1802, General Richepance, seeing

that his men were facing defeat, remembered the black soldiers of Point-à-Pitre, whom he had thrown into the holds of his ships two weeks before, and rallied them to his banners. They were led, so it seems, by a certain Pélage, a sometime educated slave, a strange mixture of pride and servility who would have gone through fire to please the white man. Delivered from the holds, driven by thoughts without salt or beauty, they went out to fight their brothers. When a soldier of the Republic fell, the nearest black traitor stripped him and donned the uniform of the European troops. Such behavior came as no surprise to Solitude and her companions, who talked it over quite calmly. But the others were bitterly disheartened, for they had never imagined that men of their own color could take up arms against them. With madness in their eyes, they smiled, wept, and smiled again. What was the use of fighting, they asked, since the black man had been damned from the beginning of time?

On the night of May 21, 1802, two days after Richepance had armed the black soldiers, the last rebels left Fort Saint-Charles by the Poterne des Galions and climbed the slopes of the volcano to the Danglemont plantation in Matouba. From all sides the defeated remnants of the insurgent forces poured into this last island of resistance, attracted by the fame of Delgrès, the leader of the insurrection, by the prospect of a last battle, a last day of brotherhood, a last taste and smell of freedom. Pushing the heavy burden of her belly before her, Solitude slowly climbed the slopes, clinging to rocks, brambles, and exposed roots. Bracing their shoulders against her loins, her companions pushed her, as though helping a mired cow out of a swamp. For two days she had been bathed in sweat; she felt as though she were walking in water, surrounded by seaweed and whirlpools and schools of little fish with fine, cutting fins. Sometimes the wave submerged her and she thrashed about with her benumbed limbs, lifting her head above the surface to breathe. Then, rediscovering Toupie and Médélices and the three Congos, she grunted deep down in her throat and murmured in a calm, playful voice, with the mysterious smile that had clung to her since Maimouni's death: "Where are all the words? Where are they?"

According to the oral tradition, they reached the heights of Matouba on the morning of the twenty-eighth, only a few hours before the end.

The plantation extended from the Black River to the Saint-Louis. The master's house on the hilltop was surrounded by a large walled-in terrace overgrown with creepers, and it was here that the rebels gathered. Passing through the silent crowd, Solitude was dimly aware of enlaced couples and of friends embracing in a last farewell: "See you in heaven, brother." They were beginning to kill the dogs, as she had seen done in Belost, Ducharmoy, and Fort Saint-Charles, for fear that these beasts who had become their friends should turn against the black man. Her companions guided her to a shed, and she sank down in its shade, stretching out her bare legs on the ground. Cries and moans rose up into the blue sky, perhaps from the unfinished child inside her, or perhaps, Solitude could not tell, simply from her own throat.

She was sitting in a river, exposed to the sun from the waist up, while her legs bathed in flowing water shot through with little fish, specks of water weed and branches that caressed her with their leafy fingers. Opening her eyes, she saw many hands around her, one resting on her cheek, another on her forehead, a third on the dripping dome of her belly. She saw faces with singularly gaping mouths and eyes that devoured her. From time to time a hand was removed from her cheeks, her forehead, her round belly and instantly replaced by another, rushing to take its place. Fingers mingled and jostled each other in the air like birds. "So you are Solitude? So it was you?" said an old Congo woman with incisions in her cheeks and long bony fingers pink with gunpowder. She seemed astonished and a trifle disappointed at finding her so pitiful, so frail and yellow and naked, so unlike the stories that had been told in the cane fields. All seemed embarrassed, some withdrew their hands, and the woman who had spoken said in a voice intended to be comforting: "It doesn't matter, my sweet, just as you are or some other way, it doesn't matter, good Lord, no, not at all; for where is the bird who can say: I look like my song? . . . where is he, I ask you?"

And as Solitude stretched out her arms, as with an effort she raised first her eyelids, then a second veil hidden beneath the first, she was suddenly immersed in the Goyave River up to her waist. Her bosom was caressed by the tall trees, while her legs and belly bathed deliciously in the cool water, among the little fish and water weeds. . . .

* * *

When she opened her eyes at about three in the afternoon, a woman's hands were massaging her with aromatic oil. Her belly was bare, her nightgown raised above her shoulders. Fish were swimming over the trees in the lost, absent sky, reflecting the wavering daylight in their scales. And instantly she awoke to this new mystery: her body on the terrace and her soul lying at the bottom of the Goyave River. Up on dry land, Toupie and Médélices were wringing their hands in anguish. They seemed to be suffocating, and weird pink tongues fluttered between their teeth, giving them a look of frantic clownish glee. Their jaws opened wide, but in vain; no sound reached Solitude's ears. Then their poor mouths closed and their lips swelled with tenderness, expressing in their way what was to be expected of Danglemont terrace: death, imminent deliverance. As the liquid mass receded, Solitude heard explosions and discovered a strip of white sky above her, as straight and pointed as a sword.

A little later as Solitude stood up and, supported by her companions, crossed the terrace to the parapet, a great light burst on the world. She saw the flash of the guns and the fountains of red earth where the balls fell. She saw children running in all directions and women dancing in a ring as they sang in tones of joy, nostalgia, and despair:

> At Morne-à-l'Eau
> At Morne-à-l'Eau
> The moon shut out the sun

Out beyond the parapet lay cane fields, slender files of indigo plants, and in the distance tall ferns that seemed to be made of crystal. As she was looking down with amazement, transfixed by the splendor of the hills descending to the sea and the sleeping harbor below, a staggering blow threw her against the parapet. She fell to her knees, her bulging belly resting on her thighs. The receding waters revealed the tattered bodies of Toupie, Médélices and the three Congos. A trickle of fine sand flowed from a cleft in the wall. Slipping one hand under her nightgown, she made sure that the liquid on her did not come from her entrails. Then a tenderness poured into her fingertips, and as though in a dream her mouth formed the words: "Just a little longer, please, just a little longer." So she remained till the end, kneeling, head erect, her belly resting lightly on her thighs. High over the mountain the sky became as vast as the sea, where all things, grass and rocks and fish, are confounded in insignificance. A shattering roar drowned out the sound of the fighting, and looking around she saw that the rebels were moving to the other side of the terrace, toward a painted chapel that stood on a rise surmounting the mansion. Out of the chapel poured an unbroken wave of black and white soldiers, all bellowing songs of France and plunging their bayonets into the mass of men, women and children, who seemed to be shouting in unison: *lan mô, lan mô, lan mô, vive lan mô* (Creole for *"La mort, la mort, vive la Mort"*). Picks, cleavers, kitchen knives clashed with the steel of the bayonets. Black women thrust their nails into the soldiers' throats, children crawled between their legs, biting the uniforms of the Republic and the bare, dark calves of the National Guards. . . .

A blond soldier ran across the terrace, his nostrils dilated with fury, his mouth bubbling with foam. At each step the plumes on his shako bobbed like a cock's crest. Solitude seized an abandoned musket and pointed it at the man with the blond curls. When she pressed the trigger, the French grenadier seemed to rise up into the air. For a moment the sky was filled with whirling rocks, with blood, with blinding light, with shimmering desolate thoughts, and then a shattering roar resounded in Solitude's belly. The Danglemont mansion had just been blown sky-high, flinging white men and black men into the same void, the same blue enchantment, the same defeat. . . .

10

ON THE VERY FIRST DAY Delgrès, the leader of the insurrection, had mined the terrace, which was to be the site of the last battle. He informed everyone of his plan, so that those willing to survive their freedom might leave. At dawn on the twenty-third, wounded by a shell splinter in the thigh, he laid a trail of gunpowder from the mine to the mansion. Then he sat down on a divan. Claude, his aide-de-camp, sat beside him. A pile of powder was placed between them, and two lighted lamps were made ready, one beside Delgrès's right leg, the other beside Claude's left leg. Three hundred rebels, Richepance's advance guard, and a large number of black women and children died in the explosion. The few survivors were carried off to prison at Basse-Terre. Captain Dauphin, found among the dead, horribly mutilated but alive, was hanged on the Cours Nolivos; then his body was displayed on the gibbet of Constantin Hill. Severely wounded in the head, Solitude was condemned to death, but not the fruit of her womb, who would become the property of her rightful owners. The sentence went unnoticed amid the wave of blood that poured over Guadeloupe. Every neck that had stuck itself out in any way was systematically severed. This included all the slaves known to have taken part in the rebellion or even in the fighting against the English, long long ago, in the days when freedom was still on the side of the Republic, and the entire mulatto class. Seized with frenzy, the whites destroyed their own patrimony. Every day, columns of sturdy field hands, each one of whom was worth as much as two thousand livres, were marched to the Cours Nolivos to be hanged. Three thousand were set down on the island rocks of Les Saintes, where their howling could be heard day and night. The survivors of Les Saintes were loaded into boats and sold on the islands of the Gulf or the Spanish territories on the mainland. Those who could not be sold were put ashore on the wild coasts of Brazil. The six hundred black National

Guards who had been taken from the holds to turn
the tide of battle were not spared, for they had
borne arms: They were sent in all haste to the
penitentiary in Brest. And among those who lived
to resume the yoke, a saying went round: "The
white man is like God; whatever you do, he kills
you."

Solitude was executed the day after her child
was delivered, on November 29, 1802.

According to one Vigneaux, a notary who had
come from Marie-Galante for that express pur-
pose, a considerable crowd attended the execution.
Some had come all the way from the British islands to celebrate the occasion. One by one, the
victims filed through the postern of the former
Fort Saint-Charles, recently renamed Fort Richepance. When Solitude appeared, the onlookers
could not believe their eyes; some merely gasped,
others made sneering remarks. She was last in
line, a pathetic old woman surrounded by four
light horsemen of the Empire. Her eyes darted in
all directions, blinking, as though wishing to see
without being seen. A tattered Creole nightgown
—green cotton dotted with rosebuds—hung down
over her nonexistent body. Under her matted

gray hair her narrow forehead stood out like a bone; her features were naked, disconnected lines. At every step, M. Vigneaux noted, she raised her knee high, which, he says, gave her an oddly disjointed look.

Unaccustomed to the daylight, she marveled at the red sun, so bright and gay, that was rising over the last moments of her life. The horses and uniforms sparkled in its light, and the yellow house fronts, the balconies, and sidewalks were swarming with people who had come to see her die. The things of this world were shrouded in a luminous veil, as fragile and beautiful as the reflections in the waters of the Goyave, and even the living bodies seemed clothed in this soft, silken transparency. Perhaps they too were reflections, parcels of the shimmering light that plunges into the Goyave. There were dresses with long trains and velvet or taffeta ribbons, and some of the young white men wore hats, cravats, and most astonishing breeches of smooth leather such as had never been seen on the island. As she passed, certain ladies of fashion jeered and tossed soft cinnamon apples, which fell on her nightgown, sending a familiar smell to her nostrils. But all those who tossed cinnamon apples were not fash-

ionable, and some of the fashionably dressed ladies tossed nothing and did not even jeer, but
merely observed her with interest. At intervals
she passed groups of field niggers, standing silent
and rigid, as though preparing for their own
execution. There were black faces and various
lighter shades; all kinds of mouths and noses,
creased foreheads, heavy, despondent eyelids,
which fell on Solitude's retina, where they were
engraved forever. Then these visions vanished,
and a street opened out on the port, revealing
sugar warehouses, gum trees, small boats, and in
the distance large sailing vessels jutting into the
blue sky. Merry-go-rounds and swings had been
set up all along the waterfront. In arbors off to one
side meringues, manioc cakes, and hot chicken
pies were for sale. The holiday atmosphere was
like the great days of the Republic, when the
blacks went to the Place de la Victoire to watch
the guillotine and see the knife fall. It was like
. . . just like . . . she said to herself in confusion, and for a brief moment a shadow of a smile
crossed her ravaged lips.

As the procession approached the Cours Nolivos, gibbets, still adorned with the corpses of the
day before, appeared among the shady tamarinds.

Cries of command rang out; the procession slowed down and stopped beside a revolving fountain. Solitude remembered a certain rumor she had heard in prison. It seemed that on previous execution days quite a few of the victims, unable to go on, had collapsed as they were approaching their destination. This had suggested a halt at the fountain, a heartening pause during which the dead niggers could drink and enjoy themselves, sprinkle each other with water and shout a last word of defiance. Then, it was found, they would resume their march to the next world with a firmer step. When at last her turn came and she bent over the fountain, a leafy twig fell at her feet. It was a fragrant, purple-flowering herb known as Christ Child, whole armfuls of which were traditionally given to young mothers. Her eyes full of tears, she looked up, wondering who had made her this offering, who on earth had had this kind thought. The first rows of onlookers consisted only of whites. But farther back in the crowd an enormous black woman in a pale blue madras was staring at her out of little round eyes, sparkling with hatred, or so it seemed. But then tears flowed down the cheeks of the woman with the madras and her features decomposed as

173

though breaking loose from their moorings. She moved her lips convulsively as if to say sh-sh. . . . Turning away from the woman with the madras, Solitude contemplated the white audience and, so the story goes, said very distinctly in an excellent French French, which startled all about her: "It seems one must never say: *Fountain, I shall not drink your water*. . . ."

Then throwing back her head and opening wide the magnificent globes of her eyes—made by the Lord, says a legend, to reflect the stars—she burst out laughing. It was a strange laugh, deep in her throat, a gentle cooing, gay and barely tempered with sadness. All the stories, all the legends and fireside tales about Solitude of Guadeloupe end with that laugh, which some likened to a song.

EPILOGUE

Today a parish road, built some years ago, rises in graceful loops bordered by flower-bedecked villas to the heights of the Matouba. Tomorrow, with the help of the tourist trade, it will be extended to the edge of the volcano, to the hot lips of the crater. After the climb from Basse-Terre, the traveler will stop a hundred yards or so from the present village of Matouba. On his left he will see a gateway, leading to a banana plantation. A guard sits silent in a kind of sentry box, and a little sign on one of the gateposts indicates that a certain Major Delgrès died within the enclosure. These guards are gentle souls. Knowing that their danger comes from the sky, they look upon men with a serene, unclouded eye. If the traveler insists, he will be permitted to visit the remains

of the old Danglemont plantation. The guard will
wave his hand, and as though by magic a tattered
black field worker will appear. He will greet the
lover of old stones with a vaguely incredulous
look, and they will start off. A long walk among
the shaggy trunks of the banana trees will take
them to a hillock overlooking the sea and the
neighboring islands, Martinique, Désirade, and
Montserrat, each of them, like Guadeloupe, surmounted by a volcano. Here they will stroll this
way and that and ultimately come to a remnant
of knee-high wall and a mound of earth intermingled with bone splinters. A wasp or two will
glitter in flight, then suddenly stop still in the
motionless air, for hummingbirds are drawn to
this remote place by the heavy scent of the hanging banana blossoms. Conscious of a faint taste
of ashes, the visitor will take a few steps at ran-
dom, tracing wider and wider circles around the
site of the mansion. His foot will collide with one
of the building stones, concealed by dead leaves,
which were dispersed by the explosion and then
over the years buried, dug up, covered over, and
dug up again by the innocent hoes of the field
workers. If he is in the mood to salute a memory,
his imagination will people the environing space,

and human figures will rise up around him, just as the phantoms that wander about the humiliated ruins of the Warsaw ghetto are said to rise up before the eyes of other travelers.

André Schwarz-Bart

André Schwarz-Bart was born in Metz to a family of Polish Jews who had arrived in France in 1924. By 1941 he was alone in the world, his parents having been taken in a Nazi roundup and deported to an extermination camp. Schwarz-Bart joined the resistance, was arrested in Limoges, escaped, and rejoined the Maquis. After the war, he worked as a mechanic, salesman, foundry laborer, miner, and librarian. In the library he developed an irresistible hunger for books. He entered the Sorbonne and turned again and again to his favorite works of literature, *Done Quixote*, *War and Peace*, the books of Thomas Mann, Stendhal, Georges Bernanos, Dostoevski and, above all, the Old Testament.

Schwarz-Bart began to write about 1950 and, in 1959, *The Last of the Just* was published. It was awarded the Prix Goncourt. He married in 1961 and, in 1967, published *Un plat de porc aux bananes vertes*, written in collaboration with his wife, Simone.